"I loved this gorgeous book abou

and refugees in a hostile city. Naseem Jamnia has created a rich, complex world in a very short space, and I am so into it. I've read a lot of books lately about empires and rulers and warfare, and it's so refreshing to read a book that's about healers. People in this book are trans, nonbinary, asexual and aromantic, and it's never a big deal but does matter to their characters, which I just adore. Firuz works as an assistant healer at a clinic run by the kindly Kofi, while teaching the novice blood-magic user Afsoneh and helping their brother Parviz to do a kind of top surgery. But a mysterious ailment is hurting people all over the city, and Firuz needs to find the cause before their fellow refugees are blamed. Jamnia deftly reveals a subtle but potent theme: when marginalized people are scared to use their power, because they're afraid others will hate them for it, bad things result. *The Bruising of Qilwa* left me wanting way more of this world and its magical systems— but above all, I wanted to spend way more time with these amazing characters. I need a whole series about Firuz, Parviz and Afsoneh. You should definitely savor this one."
—Charlie Jane Anders, author of *All the Birds in the Sky*

"Naseem Jamnia is a bold, visionary writer and *The Bruising of Qilwa* makes for a superb introduction to their nuanced and evocative Persian-inspired fantasy. The good news is that there are many more brilliant novels already in this writer's literary quiver. Get ready for them; they're coming! Jamnia is fierce and dangerous—in all the best ways."
—David Anthony Durham, author of the Acacia Trilogy

"An incredibly timely story, told by a deft hand that manages

to weave a fascinating magic system together with all-too-real issues into something truly, wonderfully, not seen before. Equal parts slice of life, fantasy tale, medical drama and mystery blend into a book not soon to be forgotten, one that should be on everyone's tbr!"
—Alice Scott, Barnes & Noble

"I adored this city, with its vibrant history and super-fresh magic system, but I loved these astonishing complex vivid characters even more. A fun and fast-paced ride that keeps you guessing all the way."
—Sam J. Miller, author of *Boys, Beasts & Men*

"With prose that reads like lush poetry, *The Bruising of Qilwa* builds an intricate world full of history, magic, and life."
—Z. R. Ellor, author of *Silk Fire*

"A fascinating medical mystery in a rich, complex world I didn't want to leave."
—Shannon Chakraborty, author of *The City of Brass*

"*The Bruising of Qilwa* transports you to a lushly described, beautifully imagined world where magic and medicine meet. Heartfelt relationships temper the grim reality of a flawed world with a creeping, strange new disease. A delightful read."
—Neon Yang, author of the Tensorate series

THE BRUISING OF QILWA

NASEEM JAMNIA

The Bruising of Qilwa
© 2022 by Naseem Jamnia

Interior and cover design by Elizabeth Story
Author photo by Jeramie Lu

Tachyon Publications LLC
1459 18th Street #139
San Francisco, CA 94107
415.285.5615
www.tachyonpublications.com
tachyon@tachyonpublications.com

Series editor: Jacob Weisman
Editor: Jaymee Goh

Print ISBN: 978-1-61696-378-1
Digital ISBN: 978-1-61696-379-8

Printed in the United States by Versa Press, Inc.

First Edition: 2022
9 8 7 6 5 4 3 2 1

To December and Phoebe, who tried to teach me to write
a short story and got this instead;
to Terry, who always believes in me;
and to Gabe, my forever reader; and

to the migrants around the world who leave their histories in search of a different future.

This book was written on traditional territories belonging to the Numu, Wašiw, Newe, and Nuwu peoples.

How many ways can you splice a history? Price a country? Dice a people? Slice a heart? Entice what's been erased back into story? My-gritude.

Have you ever taken a word in your hand, dared to shape your palm to the hollow where fullness falls away? Have you ever pointed it back to its beginning? Felt it leap and shudder in your fingers like a dowsing rod? Jerk like a severed thumb? Flare with the forbidden name of a goddess returning? My-gritude.

Have you ever set out to search for a missing half? The piece that isn't shapely, elegant, simple. The half that's ugly, heavy, abrasive. Awkward to the hand. Gritty on the tongue.

Migritude.

— Shailja Patel,
"How Ambi Became Paisley,"
from *Migritude*

I want both my countries
to be right

to fear me.

We have lost
whatever

we had to lose.

— Kaveh Akbar,
"Reading Farrokhzad in a Pandemic,"
from *Pilgrim Bell: Poems*

YEAR ONE

IN THE EARLY SUN-SWEPT HOURS of the morning, when purples and pinks smeared across the sky like blood, Firuz-e Jafari looked for a job.

It had taken a mere fifteen minutes to walk from the Underdock to their destination. Down unlit streets they stepped, keeping watch for broken glass and wooden splinters, stepping around plumped rodent carcasses, tails run over by carts or feet. The sailors and fisherfolk, up before dawn, filled the air with laughter and chatter and other sounds of their trades, interrupted but not discontinued by the muezzin's call to prayer. The briny smell of the sea and mingled odors of rotted fish and garbage faded as Firuz walked. As the crossing into the next district—the residential buffer between the largest market and the docks—transitioned from broken stones to smooth, wooden planks, Firuz's pace slowed until they found what they sought.

Over the doorway, a painted wooden sign read KOFI'S CLINIC in cracked and faded letters. Underneath, in a smaller but darker script, someone had translated it into Dilmuni, as if the Free Democratic City-State of Qilwa was still part of the queendom. Firuz's stomach backflipped, rebelled despite their lack of breakfast. Already the humid air was warm; droplets dribbled down the back of their neck. The clinic wouldn't officially open for another few hours, but if the rumors were true, Healer Kofi would already be here, readying for the day's steady stream of those who needed him. Firuz needed him, all right, though not quite in the capacity of a healer.

"The door is open," rumbled a deep voice from within. "Come in."

The voice carried over on a slight breeze, brushing past Firuz's ears like gentle lips. It brought smells of mint and ginger, which should have soothed them. Healer smells. Familiar smells. They reached to tug at a length of hair that no longer existed—they'd cut their hair the day before, in preparation for this meeting, back to its usual top crop—before pushing through, ready to persuade this Kofi person to take them on, no matter the objections.

The clinic waiting room burst with cushions and blankets, a myriad of mismatched chairs. Along the left-hand wall rose a slate board, still smudged with chalk from what might have been yesterday's patient names. The opposite wall framed a tapestry that both set Firuz's teeth on edge and made them want to hug themself. On a crimson background with golden triangles circling the edges towered the eaglelike Shahbaaz, with Ous wings outstretched, orbs clutched in Ous talons. Despite their mother's often frustrating devotion, Firuz had not worshipped in years; still, the emblem of their god was an aching reminder of the home they'd only recently left behind.

How strange, to see it in a Qilwan clinic.

Only one person stood inside, an umber-skinned individual with coils haloing their head, wearing the colorful, geometrically patterned clothes the city-state was famous for—in this case, a yellow piraahan embroidered with a repeating tear-drop boteh pattern in red, oranges, and a touch of blue. "Be right with you," they said without turning, arms kilter as they sorted herbs on a back workbench. Even from the entrance, Firuz smelled the basil flowers, noted the black sticks of licorice root in a pile to the side.

"Of course. Take your time." Firuz sat in one of the front seats, the cushion buoying their descent. They ran a hand over the fabric, soft cotton and bumps of goldoozi, embroidered flowers. No tears, not even evidence of wear. New, or cared for? Firuz doubted Kofi had discretionary funds enough to supply the clinic with new upholstery, not now. The clinics around the city were overwhelmed with plague victims, though Kofi's was the only one willing to treat the refugees fleeing from Dilmun. Refugees who had nothing, who flocked to Qilwa's streets with their terrified bodies, who brought with them—so said the argument—a disease wiping out swaths of the city, leaving behind a patchwork of neighborhoods with the sick and the healthy alike, everyone worrying they would be next.

The herb sorter soon finished, stepping over baskets on the floor towards Firuz: tall, thin, and bowed like a rice plant. Firuz remembered their manners and rose. Qilwans were big on handshakes and eye contact, unlike the Sassanian and Dilmuni tradition of kissing cheeks. "I'm sorry to barge in so early."

The other did not smile, but they did not look annoyed either. "It is no matter, as this is when I am usually here. I am called Kofi."

Did everyone in this place present themselves with only their names? How could someone look at you and assume what you wanted to be called, in a language that designated distinctions? Three weeks in Qilwa and Firuz still wasn't used to it, kept expecting the Dilmuni introduction. Fortunately, they had heard stories, knew Kofi did not care what forms of address people used, but generally acquiesced to moving through the world as a man.

"I'm they-Firuz." Reminding themself to keep firm their grip, Firuz was dismayed at the unexpectedly limp grasp of their own clammy palm. They steeled their countenance and did not wipe their hand afterward.

Kofi jutted out his chin. "Your pendant. May I?"

"Huh?" Firuz touched the golden amulet they'd worn somewhat religiously for the last year, into which they'd etched a short spell to keep bugs away. It resembled a slender dagger, its top curving into a diamond before narrowing at the hilt. The shape, a ward. The runes, a prayer. "Oh, of course." They passed it over, hiding a grimace as they did so; already they could feel the buzz of insects ganging up on them. Their skin crawled.

The healer squinted at the metal, held it up to the light. "Interesting work. Yours?"

Spots peppered Firuz's vision as their toes tingled. Could Kofi tell Firuz wasn't an adept in structural magic based on the calligraphy curving along the side? Such sloppy rune work surely outed their true magical affinity, doomed them before they'd even stated their request.

They played with the buttons on their shirt, willed the palpitations to calm, their muscles to loosen. Kofi, focused on the necklace, did not seem to notice Firuz's delay in answering. All he wanted to know was about the pendant. He hadn't asked about the magical background Firuz, as a Sassanian refugee, had to hide. "I'm—I'm a structuralist."

"That is not what I asked." Kofi covered his mouth. Something danced in his expression when Firuz caught it—annoyance, or amusement?

"Wha . . . what?" Firuz slapped the back of their neck, came away unbloodied.

Now openly smiling, Kofi raised two fingers, twirled them. A breeze began to spin around Firuz, cooling the oppressive heat. As a healer and not a physicker, Kofi had to be a magic user, more likely an adept with training, but Firuz had not heard he was an environmentalist specifically. His precise control of the breeze was a welcome surprise. Difficult, using environmental magic to heal. Interesting.

Kofi lifted the amulet back over Firuz's head unselfconsciously. "Did you make this?"

"Oh!" With the breeze and return of the necklace, Firuz's posture relaxed. Too bad it would be rude to sit while Kofi stood. "Oh, ah, yes, I did. I tend to be a mosquito's dream food." When rumors spread in Firuz's home country of Dilmun that something hunted Sassanian blood, Firuz had hastened to study structural theory. The pendant had been an early project. A fail-safe, should they need to flee. When, a year later, they did exactly that, Firuz blessed the elder who had counseled them.

Kofi tittered before clearing his throat. "Don't worry. I don't want to steal it, only admiring. It's good work, clean and steady." He bustled about, fluffing cushions, checking the supply of chalk by the board on the wall, and leaving to a back room to return with a pitcher of water, which he used to fill the samovar in the corner. The curtains over the windows he left untouched, keeping the clinic shaded. Then he turned his full attention to Firuz. "So, what can I do for you this early morning?"

Right, there was a reason Firuz was here, and not for dubitable praise. Under one loose sleeve, they dug a long thumbnail into the meat of their index. The sting reminded them of their waiting, hopeful family.

"Healer Kofi, I've come to see whether you need help in the clinic. I know the plague is spreading. I've . . . seen what it does to people."

When Firuz had arrived in Qilwa, the plague had already taken hold. Had already seized the lives of Sassanians and Dilmunis and Qilwans alike. Filled the streets with stacked bodies, bloated into the sea separating the island from Dilmun's coast. Firuz barely shut their eyes at night before the swollen faces of the dead loomed before them: the puffed and cracked lips, eyeballs bulging or else sleepy and half-lidded as though in contemplation, and the stench. The sweet, weighty smell of infection. The blooming rot of a corpse.

Kofi cupped an elbow while his other hand bracketed his chin, tapped his cheekbone. Fine lines stemmed from the corners of his mouth and eyes, though Firuz could not tell if he was ten or twenty or even thirty years older than themself. "Trained as a healer, have you?"

"Not . . . not quite. Well, yes." Firuz pulled their shoulders back, readjusted their feet to stand steady, project a confidence they didn't feel. "I was unable to complete my training, but I have enough knowledge to be an assistant. I think this plague is curable, and if anyone spent time on people other than the rich, we could get it under control."

Kofi's nostrils flared, the action darkening his otherwise pleasant features. "Ah, yes. Have you heard the governor's latest plan to streamline how healers see our patients, on suggestion of the university's scholars?"

To Firuz's shock, Kofi spat on the ground, glaring at the wad of spittle. "Migrants flood the city, an outbreak of disease happens, and what do we do? Bar the gates and hoard resources for ourselves, let people die in the streets instead of granting them a dignified passing. By those who call themselves learned people, no less." A vein pulsed in Kofi's temple. He massaged it. "Ah, there I go again, prattling about something I cannot change." He disappeared again into the back, returning with a wet rag which he used to mop up the evidence of his contempt. "Well, they-Firuz, tell me a bit about your training. I could certainly use the help."

Firuz liked how Kofi said their name; usually, the pronoun was dropped after introductions, but from Kofi it sounded affectionate, a nickname. What they did not like was the reasonable request for more information. Their prepared answers faded from their mind as though they'd numbed themself with poppy. "I— ah—did you say you work here alone?" Since Kofi had not done it, they sidled over to the samovar and opened the jar of long tea leaves behind it to dump some in the waiting pot. Potentially a good blend—aromatic and floral.

Kofi rubbed his eyes with the heel of his palm. This close, the bags under them hung heavy. "Unfortunately, the governor enticed my last assistant away to head a clinic of her own, and I am left these many months without help." He sighed as he gathered the baskets on the floor. "I don't suppose you speak Sassanian? Half of those coming in don't even know Dilmuni. My love, may hos soul soar in cloudless skies"—here Kofi's eyes flicked to the tapestry of the Sassanian god—"only taught me a little of the language before hu died, and this was many years ago, when I was still young."

Was this a test? Sweat beaded at Firuz's hairline. Skies, they'd never been this jumpy back home, but if the healer connected *Sassanian* with *training as a healer*, then *blood magic user* probably wasn't far behind. Not that Kofi would have to make those connections, as long as he looked Firuz in the eyes and knew the subtle red that rimmed them—a feature that developed in most after training, in some if their natural affinity to blood was strong. How would he take it, were he to find out? Firuz didn't know how Qilwans felt about the Sassanian science, but they feared the possibilities.

They reapplied pressure from their thumbnail to their index as they waited for the water to boil. Insofar as there were any Sassanians left from the original tribe—a feat nigh impossible after nearly a millennium of empire and three centuries of their own conquest by Dilmun—they did, theoretically, resemble Firuz. Ethnic Sassanians, though, spanned groups; besides, Sassanians and Dilmunis looked so alike with their hooked noses and range of olive skin tones and thick, dark brown or even black hair. Firuz could admit their own linguistic knowledge without revealing more.

Strange, though, about the others not speaking what should have been their second tongue. Modern Sassanian, as a spoken language, was speckled with

Dilmuni, and the people who still knew it—blood adepts and rural folk, mostly—were almost always bilingual. After all, Dilmun was their home. Well, had been their home.

"You know," Firuz ventured, lifting the spigot to pour water into the teapot when the *glug* of boiling began, "they might be afraid of you."

"Afraid?" Kofi tilted his head, hand poised to pick up the baskets he'd been filling with sorted plants. "Why would they be afraid? I'm a healer, not whatever is hunting them across the sea."

Firuz flinched so hard, they nearly dropped the teapot. One thing to know the current fate of their people, another to hear the careless mention tossed out like trash to be burned. Taking a deliberately slow, deep breath against their rising heart rate, they stacked the pot on top of the samovar and searched for a towel to cover it. Finding none, their wild pulse now demanding acknowledgment, they pressed two fingers to their neck, willing it to calm. "They don't know you, Kofi-khan. They don't know whom to trust." Kofi turned, lips pursed, trying to balance two piles of baskets; Firuz hovered for a beat before stepping forward to take one. "Where does this go? Do you have something to cover the tea with?"

"Back room with the blue curtain. We can grab a towel from there as well." Kofi shifted the remaining baskets onto a hip, as if the tower were a child, without toppling the precious cargo. "You raise an interesting point, they-Firuz. Let's see what else you can do."

The first food riot happened a month after Firuz started working in Kofi's clinic. Another flood of migrants spun the city into a panic, and the needy who weren't already sick began to starve. For five days, the two worked far past the usual hours as injured rioters poured through, filling the air with the dense smell of sweat, the high pitch of moans. Firuz took to spending the night in case someone came stumbling to the door at unexpected times, which happened more than once.

Even after the city guard—a recently designated group the governor had cobbled together from former freedom fighters—quelled the unrest, those affected, in addition to the plagued sick, came to the clinic in the hopes of some kind of help. On principle or out of desperation, some laborers traveled from across the city, despite the presence of closer clinics, trekking hours to seek an Academy-trained healer whose justice, in the form of his practice, included the poor.

For three weeks, Firuz and Kofi distributed the foodstuffs given to them in payment to those who needed them more. Firuz did not tell Kofi their family needed help too; instead, at the end of the day, they scraped together the remains to send with their younger brother, who would stop in on the way home from lessons. The number of days they slept on the clinic sofa without a meal in their belly ticked ever higher.

At the end of a light day, an unexpected boon, Kofi stopped Firuz as they folded clean bandages, their hands cracked and dry. "I expect you to go home today, they-Firuz."

"Hm?" Firuz yawned despite themself, then opened and closed their mouth several times in disgust at the sour taste at the back of their throat.

"Things are calming down. I want you to take to-morrow to rest with your family." When Firuz pro-tested, Kofi squeezed their shoulder. "I mean it. An exhausted healer is a useless one. I cannot have my partner getting sick on me."

Partner. The praise jolted down Firuz's spine, and they flushed. "Thank . . . thanks, Kofi-khan. Are you—"

"Yes, yes, I'm sure!" Kofi shooed Firuz towards the entrance. "I am also sure your mother and brother miss you. Go home! Go sleep. I'll see you in a couple of days. Oh, wait—" Kofi ducked around the table at the front, where he lifted up a basket. A draped cloth hid the contents. "Take this with you. I will not take no for an answer."

Quite a haul: two sesame barbari flatbreads, prob-ably only a day or two old; a jar of pickled vegetable torshi; a handful of dried chickpeas; three bright toma-toes; a couple small, dark red chilies—which neither Sassanian nor Dilmuni cooking used, but had been incorporated into Qilwan dishes when merchants had brought the plant to the island some decades back—and four long eggplants, enough to make a khoresht, if only there were rice or lamb. Was it so obvious their family was starving? Over the weeks, Firuz had tried to let their guard down around Kofi, but the two had been too busy for much personal chatting. Firuz mumbled a thanks and dipped through the clinic door, eager to collapse on a real mattress.

The clinic hugged the edge of the neighborhood past the bazaar, midway between the latter and the Underdock. No lanterns illuminated the streets yet; the sunlight streamed through the trees as clouds gathered in the distance. The air was more damp than usual, ladened with the scent of impending rain. Eager to avoid the deluge, Firuz hurried down the streets.

Deep in the heart of the dock slums, the hovel they lived in—Firuz refused to call it a house, not when they'd soon be able to afford one even a modicum better—waited among the other shanties. Firuz picked their way across debris-strewn streets, cold water soaking into their thin shoes. Gross. When they'd packed up their family to flee to Qilwa, they hadn't been so naive to believe it would be easy, that they'd arrive in anything but relative poverty. Still, the contrast between the small farming village in which they'd been raised and the wet Underdock, the constant stink of mildew and garbage, the rattling of lungs warning of the plague—sometimes, Firuz wanted to curse the dark hole Qilwa had relegated their people to and go back to Dilmun, where there were blessedly limited mosquitoes. Fortunately, some Sassanians, particularly those of mixed descent, could live in better neighborhoods, passing for something other-than.

Firuz gingerly lifted the slab of wood serving as a door and stepped inside. The low ceiling forced them to stoop. Their mother had already lit the evening candles, which cast flickering shadows in their halos, and Firuz used the light and their outstretched hand to guide their way down the narrow corridor and to the room serving as the family everything. Dark, dank, and cramped, what with the sharing of the structure with another family, nothing redeemed this place.

No nap for Firuz: Parviz sat beside the sole bed, the plank used as the family table placed atop it. He resembled Firuz—shorter, but with the same broad hips and soft, spacious belly. He looked more and more like Firuz each day as his eyebrows bushed, his skin darkening from dusk to a light bronze, making Firuz feel their age, shy yet of three decades.

Parviz looked up from his book and smiled. "How was work?" Thank the skies, but his voice still had the pitch of youth to it.

"Busy." Firuz heard the exhaustion in their own voice. Over two months at the clinic and it seemed half the slums showed up on a daily basis. "Where's Maadar?"

"Hamaam. She said she didn't want to insult God by showing up before Ou unclean." Parviz rolled his eyes.

Firuz tried to hide their smile but failed. "She wanted you to go with her, didn't she?"

Parviz gripped their pen, might have snapped it had Firuz not wriggled it from his grip. Pens were expensive. "Can't you get her to stop? She listens to you!"

"Not for long. Try calling her naneh; she hates being reminded of her age." She'd borne her children late in life; perhaps she saw Firuz aging and felt the same way they did about Parviz. Firuz perched atop the makeshift table, picked up Parviz's reading material. A disgusted noise escaped them. "Really, you're reading this garbage? Abbaass is notorious for not giving other cultures their due. All he does is celebrate our history, as if it's only ours." The base of Firuz's head, where it connected with their neck, ached with restrained tension. "What is this golaabi school?"

Parviz stuck his tongue out. "Not everyone gets a quality Dilmuni education like you."

Not everyone lived in a country requiring education for everyone, regardless of ethnicity, either. To Qilwa's credit, their short independence had seen other priorities attended to first. "Your teacher is Dilmuni; ey should be giving you a quality education." Parviz's stomach gurgled at the same time Firuz's did, cutting off further fuss. "Guess I'll go make dinner."

Parviz leaned over to see what Firuz had brought home, lifting the cloth covering the basket before dropping it as if stung. "Akh! Eggplant!"

"It'll grow on you. Besides, look what else came with it." Firuz plucked out the tomatoes, their fresh, leafy smell wafting with the movement. Parviz's face brightened, to Firuz's pleasure. "Thought that would make you happy. You keep reading your muck-awful book—"

"Good thing Maadar didn't hear that."

"—and I'll go cook." They jerked their thumb towards the door. "Are the others here?" There was barely enough food for the three of them, let alone for the four others residing in the next room. Firuz struggled constantly whether their family should suffer more to feed morsels to another. It was hard enough to make sure none of them got sick, scorching away any hint of illness daring to step inside.

Parviz shrugged. "They weren't earlier. What are you making? Do you need help?"

"You still have homework." Firuz tapped the cover of the book before pushing themself off the table. "Can't get out of it on my account." They leaned down to nuzzle their nose into Parviz's hair, inhaling the lingering soap smell. "I do have one bit of good news. One of Kofi's old university friends gave us a bunch of books. One of them has a whole chapter on alignments."

Parviz's entire face changed: the tired sag of his eyes widened, his thick brows lifted, his lips parted. "Really?"

"I'll get to work on the spell as soon as I can." Firuz nodded to the binding vest hanging on the side of the bed, a hand-me-down from before their own alignment. They'd kept it out of a weird sense of nostalgia, and their brother had requested it before they'd all left Dilmun. "Then you won't have to wear that anymore. Although we can start on the ointment sooner rather than later; that shouldn't be too complicated to make. We'll have to fiddle with the dose to get your facial hair not to grow in patchy." Parviz did have a light sweeping of hair already along his lips and chin and cheeks, and though the strands were dark, the softness countered a starker appearance. "I might be able to make a distillate, too, to deepen your voice."

Parviz pressed himself into his sibling's shirt. He probably thought it hid the tremors of his shoulders. Firuz rubbed his back. "Thanks, Rooz."

"What, you're thanking me now?" Firuz kissed his sweaty forehead before peeling away. "Thank me when your homework is done and when the spell works."

"Yeah, yeah." Parviz turned away, though Firuz saw the glint of tears anyway. They stretched, careful of the ceiling, glad they might be able to do something right amid everything else out of their control.

The heat from the brick oven tucked in the alleyway danced on Firuz's skin. Mask and gloves in place, they mouthed a traditional send-off before heaving the body into the waiting flames. It was not a healer's job to dispose of the dead, but over the past few weeks, the distinction between mortuary and clinic had, for these purposes, faded. The oven was scant fingers large enough to fit the corpse, and Firuz's navel pinched before they squashed the feeling—and the body—down. They had no choice. Disposing of the plague victims in any other way invited further disease.

They snapped off their gloves and mask and tossed those into the fire, too, before shutting the oven door. "That's the last of them, Kofi-khan," they called when they returned inside. "We can close up now." Their belly rumbled its eagerness to depart.

"Not quite." The curtain leading to the examination rooms pulled back, and Kofi poked his head out. "Come back here for a moment."

"What's going on?"

Kofi gestured down the hall. "We have a visitor."

In the furthest room, where they usually stored equipment and mixed treatments, stood a familiar grim-faced mortician. Hair shorn since the last time Firuz had seen her, wearing the tight black garb of a person who didn't want their sleeves caught in their oft-unclean work, Mortician Malika had worked closely with Firuz over the weeks, as Kofi's was the closest clinic "whose healers don't have asses for brains." She also once told Firuz she worked with the dead because she wanted to avoid dealing with the complaints of the living.

The plague had turned everything on its head.

"Malika-khan, what brings you here?" Her attention flicked towards them and back, and Firuz followed her gaze to the raised sheet stretched over an examination bed that usually did not reside there. "Is that a . . . person?"

"Technically, a corpse." She crossed her arms. "I was hoping an adept might make sense of this."

"Not another plague victim, then?"

"If it is, then the plague has changed, and we're mucked."

Despite the progress made over the last many months—getting people from all parts of the city access to clean water; a volunteer band of magic users who went through the streets and destroyed any waste that might contribute to disease; a recent donation by one of the wealthy merchant families of much-needed food—up the death toll still ticked. If more migrants arrived from Dilmun, the city would be in even more trouble, especially if the ancient Aziza Kiwabi Academy continued to oppose their entry on the grounds of "public health."

Firuz grabbed the gloves Kofi offered, although he wasn't wearing any. "Kofi-khan?"

"We already talked about it." As was his habit, Kofi motioned with his chin to Malika, whose arms were crossed. "I did a preliminary exam, and I don't want to bias either of us. Let's hear what you see."

Firuz's hand hesitated by a mask. Eight months working with Kofi, and Firuz had learned it was safe to relax around him. During their training in Dilmun, they'd been subjected to constant tests of skill, but Kofi trusted Firuz. He insisted they were well trained, needed only experience to call themself a full healer. But something about this felt . . . off. Perhaps it was the furrow in Kofi's brow, or the way he wouldn't look directly at the corpse but instead focused on his dark hands.

Well, regardless, Firuz's duty lay with the person awaiting them, living or dead.

After snapping on the mask, they folded the sheet away from the corpse's face. "I take it I should not ask what's unusual about this one." Seemed normal enough; they fingered the sagging jaw, the bloated cheeks, before pulling the sheet further down.

Malika pulled up her own mask from around her neck for sake of the imminent smell. "I can tell you it's the fourth one in this state, and it's unlike anything I've ever seen."

The stomach, already green with the telling patch of decay, distended around their touch. Gases expelled into the air, smelling of sulfurous rotten eggs and sun-heated garbage. Firuz turned their cheek to breathe in the scent of dried herbs the mask had been nestled in as Malika coughed. Kofi waved a hand in front of his face.

Firuz was familiar with decayed bodies along with live ones. They didn't need to access their magic to feel something about this one was very, very wrong.

Under normal circumstances, the gut spilled into the blood, consumed the body from the inside out. The marrow no longer cranked out new life, and over time, only bones remained. The marrow here was doing . . .

*some*thing, even though it should have long been still.

"How long has this one been dead?" Firuz retrieved surgical tools. The putridity—or rather, the lack of it, after the initial discharge—concerned them.

Malika bounced a fist against her thigh. "One week."

Firuz's head snapped up. "Excuse me?"

The bouncing stopped, and she slid her hands into pockets and bowed her head. Such behavior belied her usual confidence. "That's why I brought it here."

At one week, the body should have been well into decay, its odor a mix of wet rot, too-ripe fruit, and rancid meat. The initial gases had resembled that bouquet of scents, but there was no real skin slippage as Firuz pinched the arm, no telltale yellow marbling. It was as though the body had begun its decay, then stopped, or had picked parts of the process to continue the way a farmer picked dates.

Their blade slid through the chest like a ripe mango, the skin curling as the pressure released. Firuz suppressed a gag. The body was rotting, all right, although the outside didn't mirror the internal goo. Firuz used a rag to wipe down the flat bone connecting the ribs before tapping it, but did not hear the expected hollow-ish ring. "Kofi-khan, can you—"

Kofi already held out the handsaw, then flipped the skin back so Firuz could work. "You suspect the marrow?"

"Maybe. Something is stopping full putrefaction." They did not elaborate, did not want to utter the fears nipping at the small of their back.

31

In normal circumstances, bones were home to spongy crisscrosses of red or yellow fibers, the site of blood-making marrow. As a person aged, so, too, did the composition of these fibers change. Yet those here were dense, resembling a newborn babe's. A chunk of sternum in hand, Firuz stepped to the magnifying lens set on the back counter, but there was a more precise way to puzzle out what was happening. With their back to the others, they freed the tip of the needle sewn in their sleeve and pressed it to their wrist until a drop of blood welled up.

Blood would tell, as it always did.

Red smeared against white, they used the energy surging through their veins to explore the bone's makeup, even as they pressed their cheekbones into the eyepiece of the lens. The magic allowed them to feel the internal structure, run invisible hands along the matrix inside. The blood still present felt wrong, lacking something, and the bone was too thin, as if eroded away. And the marrow? Most of it was silent, but a part of it thrummed, even now trying to create without the prerequisite ingredients.

Which was . . . impossible. The person was dead, literally cut open by Firuz's own hands. Still, the bone whispered its life, its desire to create. No, there was something—or someone—behind this, playing with bodies with a carelessness or disregard that twisted Firuz's insides.

Earlier, they'd been hungry; their appetite had long since fled, and without the exam, they didn't know where to settle. "What did you feel when you checked?"

Kofi moved one hand over the open chest cavity as his other directed the spinning waterwheel in the corner, from which he drew his energy. The gooey innards shifted in tandem. "Viscous like it should be. No stirring of the muscles. Dead, but not yet decayed." He dropped the motion.

Malika tapped her toes in a rhythm Firuz could almost place. Back to her usual self, then. "So, any thoughts?"

"Some kind of preservation spell, with maybe food as the medium." The lie slipped out without a second thought as they dumped their tools in a bucket and reached for the mixture of herbs bundled for a cleansing solution. "Though why someone is preserving bodies is beyond me."

"Hm." Malika scratched her scalp as she considered. "Grave robbers, perhaps? Maybe some of the other free states see this as an opportunity for their physickers."

"Foolish," dismissed Kofi. He wrapped the body with the sheet, securing it with tight knots. "Risk their trainees getting sick?"

Malika toyed with her sleeve, plucking and twisting the cloth. "Honestly, I'd consider it in their shoes. Use the distraction of the plague to sneak out other bodies. Great way to learn. Best way, really."

"Unethical." Kofi's smile was cold as he finished his work. Stronger than he looked, he hefted the body onto his shoulder. "Clever, maybe, but the bodies deserve better treatment."

Malika nodded. "I don't disagree, but times of strife create unique opportunities."

"In any case," Firuz interrupted, needing to go boil water for their instruments, "I'd burn them as they come in and not worry about it. We all have enough on our plates as it is."

Malika sighed, then grabbed the bottom half of the wrapped corpse so Kofi wouldn't have to carry it out alone. "Guess that's all we can do. Keep watch for me, will you? I want to monitor the situation."

"Of course."

The truth was, thought Firuz as they washed their hands, this was the work of the most incompetent blood magic user they'd ever seen.

When the governor, with her Academy-trained physickers' blessings, declared the plague to be over—no new cases had happened in over two weeks, not even with the latest arrival of migrants from Dilmun—the city celebrated. The merchant district gathered supplies, shops opened their doors, the largest market district closed its stalls for the day, and a grand party for all filled the streets with laughter and relief. Even the scholars emerged from their towers from across the island, opening their courtyards and gardens for public perusal.

The next food riot happened a few weeks later. The governor retreated to her manor as refugees marched up the hill to petition at her gates. Fury from not only the migrants but poor Qilwans resounded in the streets after such a recent, lavish display of the wealth sitting in the city's treasury. The resulting violence, courtesy of the guard, left behind dozens of brutalized bodies for the morticians to bury. Meanwhile, Kofi's clinic brimmed with injured survivors when yet another set of laws further limited noncitizens' access to care. Despite the presence of at least a dozen around the city, Kofi's was quickly becoming the last free clinic in Qilwa.

Firuz ran their fingertips along the hardened tissue near their belly button as they walked home from, hopefully, the last of the riot victims. Ten months in Qilwa, and they hoped, though were not naive enough to believe, it would be the last of the unrest. At least, for a while.

So lost in thought were they that, at first, the watery coughs didn't register. Their feet stilled as the coughs continued, and they swiveled, hunting the source. They traced the noise back to an alleyway. It was not much more than a dark gap between buildings, overhung with a melancholic odor of garbage. Firuz covered their nose with their sleeve as they headed down.

The alley ended with a neighboring home's brick wall. Firuz knelt by a wobbling pile of dirty rags.

"Anyone in there?" They kept their voice gentle, as if talking to a startled animal.

The answer came as another series of coughs—lung-water, from the sounds of it.

"It's okay; I'm not here to hurt you. I'm a healer."

At that, a small face peered out from under a scrap of cloth, covered in scratches and dirt. Dull brown eyes gleamed almost reddish in the shadows, blinking at them.

Those irises—too similar to their own. Firuz pushed the thought away. "Hi there. What's your name?"

More blinking, a wary squint, then: "It's . . . she-Afsoneh."

Oh. *Oh.* A child no older than fifteen, Parviz's age; the introduction; the tinted ring around her irises. Firuz switched to a language that came naturally to them and likely did to her too. "Afsoneh-jan, do you have family here?"

The spoken Dilmuni, with the Sassanian suffix, was enough. She pushed aside the tattered blanket, sat up so matted hair tumbled into her face. Another cough, an impatient swipe at the strands, before her sharp focus snapped onto Firuz. The scraps around her were so filthy they crinkled when she rubbed them. "You're like me, aren't you?" She didn't switch to Sassanian, so Firuz assumed she didn't know it. "Who are you?"

"I'm they-Firuz. Like I said, I'm a healer." The Sassanian welcome was "it's good you've come," but given the circumstances, that felt inappropriate. Instead, Firuz extended a hand. "Why don't you join my family for dinner? My brother is around your age, I think; I'm sure he'd love to meet you. He doesn't have a lot of friends." They were banking on the shared ethnicity, in this city of all places, to be enough for this child to trust them—and not think it the Sassanian back-and-forth etiquette of taarof, with its repeated offers and expectations of refusal. Another place, another life, another Firuz might not have bothered, but this Firuz, in Qilwa, had little recourse.

She stared at their hand, with its cut nails and calluses, instead of taking it. "I'm not exactly presentable, and I don't have anything for . . . for deedani." The word was awkward on her tongue, as if not spoken often, reaffirming Firuz's guess about her linguistic knowledge. No one would fault her for coming to a home empty-handed, yet here she was, laying it out as a concern.

"I'm not good at taarof, Afsoneh-jan." Firuz plucked at their sweaty piraahan. "I need to wash up, too. Why don't we go to the garmaabeh first?" At the confused look, they amended to the Dilmuni: "Hamaam." Afsoneh cleared her throat, then spat. Her hand came away with a glob of yellow mucus. Firuz grimaced. "We need to take care of that. We can go to the bathhouse, and then I can heal you back at my home. Or, if you don't like that idea, we do have a small tub. Not great for a proper bath, but it'll be private."

Cool air rushed through the alley. Firuz peeled their shirt away from their torso to allow airflow, fanning themself. Afsoneh scratched her nose. Firuz stilled their fidgeting, despite the pinch in their hip.

Finally, she pushed the makeshift blanket away and rose. She was far too skinny and had a pus-swollen sore on her arm. Firuz rose from their crouch, wincing, and again offered their hand, which Afsoneh took this time. The clammy touch was enough to confirm Firuz's earlier suspicion: her blood rose to dance with theirs, a harmony that sang in their veins. They did not meet her curious expression. The two of them could talk about what it meant after she'd been healed.

As they walked back into the street, Afsoneh using her free hand to shield herself from the light, Firuz took stock of her state. More injuries along her legs; her hair wasn't only matted but teeming with lice. Her clothes would have to be destroyed. Luckily, her nails weren't blue; the lung-water must not have progressed far, thank the skies. The two stayed silent on the walk back, the sun beginning its descent in the background, storm clouds drawing closer.

Firuz led Afsoneh to the edge of the dock district, where they'd moved their family into a cottage a couple of months ago. The new home was farther from work than the last one, but it was worth it. What a relief to live in their own space, where their mother could have a corner altar and Parviz a real table at which to study. Shame flooded Firuz whenever they thought of the nearby Underdock, of the other family in their old living situation. How could Firuz take care of their own and ignore the suffering they'd left behind, the suffering they condoned every time they chose their family over others?

The clinic—they could do more good there than sharing what few resources they had. They had to justify it to themself this way or risk the guilt consuming them, a disease of its own.

Firuz opened the door of their home and led Afsoneh through. She hugged herself, standing in the kitchen, as Firuz checked to see if anyone was in. Although the perfume of esfand lay thick in the air, no smoke rose from the altar. The rooms were empty too. "Are you hungry? Wait, no. Silly question." They grabbed that morning's leftover sangak from the breadbasket, then opened the icebox for feta, the pantry for dates and pistachios. Then a clay cup for water. "Help yourself to the fruits in the basket on the table. I'll go heat the bath."

Afsoneh, following their movements, accepted the offered sustenance. "Thank you."

Firuz observed the hurried bites, the attempts to slow herself, and fumbled for words before deciding to do as they said they would. Grabbing and lighting a candle on the way, they went to the wash closet, knelt to fill the bath from the pump they'd paid a fortune to install, and heated the water with the runes they'd painted at the base of the tub, drawing energy from the flame. Not the best source, but it did the trick, even if it did melt the wax down to a warm puddle pooling on Firuz's skin. Afterward, they grabbed a towel, some of Parviz's clothes—no doubt loose on

Afsoneh, as malnourished as she appeared—and soap. When they came back out, Afsoneh had finished eating and was peeking around. The cottage was simple, but clean and stable: three rooms in addition to the kitchen and bathroom, the walls plain and unadorned for now.

It was more than what those in the Underdock had, and Firuz seethed with the knowledge.

"I'll set up what I need here," they said from the living room. Blanketed by a rug they'd filched from a trash heap and painstakingly cleaned, the room hosted a shelf of books, a table with a few chairs, and cushions against the wall for seating. Firuz pushed the table to the wall to create an empty swath of space, perfect for magic. They gestured to the bathroom. "Everything you need should be in there. When you're done, pull the stopper from the drain."

Afsoneh quivered as she curled in on herself. "Can you . . . cut my hair first?"

"Oh." Firuz lifted a hand towards her, waited for permission. When she nodded, they ran it through the coarse clumps. "I'll have to shear it all off if I do." Doing so had the added benefit of allowing them to kill off whatever burrowed there.

To her credit, her voice was steady. "Please."

It did not take long. Firuz spread an old tablecloth beneath them. Afsoneh held her head high and trembled, palms in her lap, when the brown mats, blackened with dirt, fell to the ground. She retreated to the bath as Firuz swept the strands into what had been a sofreh sheet and folded it to the side; along with her old clothes, they'd take the bundle to the clinic the next day to burn.

After setting the kettle to boil, they spread a new sheet and set out the contents of their healer's bag. The lung-water would be straightforward to heal, but it spelled a conversation about their tandem-shifting blood, their shared red-rimmed eyes. Firuz knew a blood magic user when they felt one, and despite her irises, she'd had none of the scars indicative of adept training—which meant, since there were no elders here, it was up to Firuz to make sure she received it. A responsibility they did not need right now.

The front door opened as Firuz finished setting up. "Naneh?" called Parviz's voice.

"Not home." Firuz settled on their knees, although it was not the most comfortable position. "Though we do have a guest. C'mere a moment."

Some shuffles preceded Parviz's appearance. He munched a piece of plum lavaashak Firuz had picked up from the one Sassanian vendor in the affordable section of the bazaar, who hid zher ethnicity with Qilwan heritage. "Who's the guest?"

Firuz motioned him closer.

"What?"

Parviz spoke Sassanian at home, Dilmuni outside— he was still learning Qilwan—and with Afsoneh's suspected lack of knowledge of their native tongue, Firuz stuck to the same language so she wouldn't over- hear. "She's taking a bath. I want to talk to you."

Their brother tugged on his ear, checking around him, before mimicking Firuz's posture beside them. Unlike the younger Jafari's, Firuz's body was not flexible, and whereas Parviz could sit on his knees for hours without feeling the strain, Firuz could not. "Why is someone taking a bath in our house?" he asked.

"She's one of us." Even if Afsoneh couldn't translate, they spoke in a low tone. "I don't think she has a family. I'm going to offer her a place here."

Parviz buzzed his lips.

Their mother would have been appalled. Firuz was a little appalled himself when they channeled her: "Cheh loos."

Parviz mocked the words calling out his immaturity by repeating them with a head wag. "I thought we escaped having to live with other people."

"She's your age. I think you'll like her." Firuz nodded to the sofreh they were both sitting on. It wouldn't be used for eating after this, that was for sure. "She's sick. It might help her to have someone else here during the healing."

Parviz contemplated this, hand going to the angry pimple on his chin, before brightening. "Does this mean I don't have to do homework?"

The audacity of adolescence. "It means a delay. Stop picking; it's not ready yet."

"Ugh." Parviz scooted to sink into the cushions and crossed his legs. "Fine."

Quiet footsteps against the wooden slats of the floor announced Afsoneh's presence. She seemed relaxed in

Parviz's clothes. As Firuz had predicted, they swallowed her frame; still, she looked warm, and it was better than the rags she'd been wearing and was now carrying. Firuz held out their hands.

As she passed her bundle over, Afsoneh noticed Parviz. Pink dusting her cheeks, a sandy olive paler than both Jafari siblings, she dropped her gaze almost as hastily as her old clothes. Parviz pushed up against the wall and also studied the floor. Firuz looked from one to the other and bit back a smile. They might not have such feelings of their own—romance was not only foreign to them but completely uninteresting— but they could appreciate a spark between others. "Afsoneh," they said, going back to Dilmuni. "This is my brother, he-Parviz. Parviz, this is she-Afsoneh."

Afsoneh reached as if to tuck a loose strand of hair, but when her fingers met skin, she dropped it. "Hi."

Parviz rubbed his nose with an open palm. "Hi. Uh—are those my clothes?"

"Oops," said Firuz, unapologetic.

"Oh—I'm sorry, I didn't know—"

"Uh, no, it's okay, really—"

Both exasperated by and amused with the distraction of teenaged awakenings—another thing Firuz thankfully avoided; puberty had shown them that unlike some of their peers, sex was about as desirable as a maggot-infested banana—Firuz patted the sofreh. "Come, sit. We have some healing to do." Afsoneh recoiled, but when Firuz didn't budge, she joined them, ducking her head before Parviz could notice her staring. "Go ahead and lie down," said Firuz. She complied, and they picked up a rag doused in alcohol to rub down their scalpel. "I imagine you know what I'm going to do now."

She wrung her hands. "Cut out my lungs?"

"What? No!" Firuz couldn't tell if she was joking. Parviz laughed, and had he been sitting closer, Firuz would have elbowed him. "I'm going to access to your blood. A small cut on both of us. Have you ever been healed before?" She shook her head. "Then this will probably feel invasive, like someone crawling under your skin. Try not to fight it, and I'll try to make it quick. Deal?"

She squinted at the blade. "Will it hurt?"

"Not too bad, but I can put you to sleep before I begin." An awakened state was more ideal, so Firuz could receive constant feedback as to the result of their work, but at this point, they were more interested in healing the poor girl than prolonging her misery.

Clutching her stomach, Afsoneh watched the ceiling. "Can I, uhm. Ask some—some questions about ma—about what you're going to—you know." She shot Parviz a nervous glance.

Ah. At least she knew to be cautious. "Oh. Yes, he knows. You can talk freely. I want to discuss that too. But first—" Firuz sliced open the meat of their palm, the sting waking them. It was one of the most painful places to cut, but it also meant plentiful access to their magic via the blood flow, which meant quicker healing.

She fixated on the flow down Firuz's wrist. "I—ow!"

Firuz put down the scalpel and picked up Afsoneh's bleeding hand with their own. What was it the elders used to say to their child trainees? They were clouds full of rain? Yeah, Firuz was not going to say that. "Sorry. Hopefully that's the most painful part." They pressed their hand against hers, felt the blood mingle.

With this method, it was so easy for her body to give an account of what was happening to it and the steps Firuz had to take. First, kill off the lice eggs on her head. Then, the wounds on her legs, the gift of some scurrying animal: choke off the nutrients the blood provided to the infection, clean out the dead tissue, and seal the vessels and knit the skin. Yes, easy.

"I thought you said it wouldn't hurt," said Afsoneh between clenched teeth.

"I say that every time," said Parviz, who'd at some point retrieved embroidery cloth, needle, and thread to work diligently alongside his sibling.

It shouldn't have been painful, not to her. Pain meant what Firuz had suspected. "You've never been trained, have you?"

She shook her head, the skin around her forehead and eyes twitching as she closed them. "My medars didn't like the way the elders did things. I was never registered."

"Does that mean you don't speak Sassanian?" Parviz looked intrigued. In their small village, everyone had spoken the language, and he'd never gotten a chance to visit one of the big cities where it was a rarity.

Even with her eyes closed, the discomfort was clear on Afsoneh's face, although that might have been from the healing. "I know some words. My medars could understand it but didn't speak it themselves."

Finally, an opportunity to broach this subject. "Your parents," Firuz asked, "where are they now?"

"Gone." She said it without a trace of emotion. "But I know it's important to train. Umi knew some environmental stuff, so zhe tried to teach me to use water. It's been hard. I mean, I only started doing anything with blood a couple of years ago."

In the background, the kettle began to whistle. Parviz dropped his sewing to take care of it before Firuz could ask; bless brothers. "And how old are you?"

"Fourteen."

Like the tailor their mother had once been, the profession their brother had recently shown an interest in, Firuz sewed together the last of the blood vessels on Afsoneh's legs. "Most begin blood magic training by eight or nine." Precocious students often began younger, though Firuz disagreed with that practice. "You didn't feel anything by then?"

Afsoneh gnawed on her lip until the cracks on them bled. Firuz indulged her what must have been a habit. "Medar said hu got someone to brand me when I first started showing signs. Hu had it removed when it started to hurt."

"Mucked-up skies." A brand was every adept's worst nightmare. "Afsoneh, I'm . . . I'm sorry." Firuz awkwardly covered one of her hands with their clean one.

"The elders' methods are painful, yes, but they give you control. Teach you limits."

"I think they were afraid, my medars." Afsoneh's legs jittered against the cloth, would have rattled a table had she been on one. "Firuz, will you train me? Please? I . . . I can't pay, but—"

"Yes, of course I'll train you." Firuz followed the looping system of blood vessels to her lungs. Pockets that should have been filled with air were instead ripe with wet pus. "I'm no teacher and certainly not an expert, but I can give you the basics."

Afsoneh hissed as Firuz prodded the blood to eat away at the infection swimming in the area. Blood would always tell, and its capacity to heal the body and fight off disease would forever impress them. What else could it do that they'd yet to discover? "I would say thank you," Afsoneh said, "but this still hurts."

"Hurts now, but you'll feel like someone melted nabaat in your veins soon enough." Now there was a saying Firuz hadn't thought of in years.

"Nabaat belongs in tea, not blood." Parviz leaned against the wall. "And speaking of, tea's steeping."

"Tea sounds great right now," managed Afsoneh between gasps.

"I promise I'm almost done." Firuz tried to numb the pain, but that was a skill they still needed to practice. Precious little time to do so, and besides, in the clinic, they only used structural magic. Maybe they should start stocking up on healing herbs at home; surely Kofi's greenhouse had plenty to spare. "We have two other considerations. One is a matter of where you'll stay. We don't have the space for your own room, but I could set up a private area in this one, if you don't want to share ours."

Afsoneh swiveled her head at them, then back to look up at Parviz, who was still standing. He squirmed under her attention. "If your parents are gone, where else are you going to go? Maadar spends most of her days at the shrines anyway. And Firuz is okay to live with, I guess, when they're home."

Heat climbed up Firuz's neck, though the callout was fair. "Thanks for the glowing praise. We have the space for you, but take some time to think about it; you're welcome to stay here until you decide. And the last thing: school. You can join Parviz." Though it wasn't much of one—a teacher ran lessons for a small group, across varying ages, in the back of a bookshop. Almost a year in Qilwa, and there still wasn't a proper school that would accept Parviz. It annoyed Firuz to no end.

Afsoneh balked, shuffling in place, and perhaps not from healing. "School!"

"Oh c'mon Rooz, you're going to force her to go to school?" Parviz settled back in his earlier spot. "I thought you said it was a golaabi school anyway."

"You both still have to go. If I'm going to train you, I want you to have the most normal life you can otherwise."

Parviz barked a laugh. "Nothing about our lives here is normal." He could have sounded grim or bitter.

He could have blamed the uprooting of their Dilmu-ni lives on one person's abilities. But Firuz heard only nonchalance in their brother's voice. Still, their relief was a tempered one.

Afsoneh grinned at Firuz. The genuine joy brought out the apples in her cheeks, the sparkle in her eyes, and in another life, that was what she should have looked like, instead of a child half-starved and half-dead. "I like him."

"Good. The two of you can look after each other." The whole prospect lightened Firuz's mood. They hated how Parviz came home after school radiating dejection, without friends, missing home—wherever home was now. The potential of this friendship with someone Firuz wanted to monitor anyway fed two birds with one loaf. Perhaps their family would be able to embrace this new life after all, without losing everything they'd once held dear.

Firuz traced the cut on Afsoneh's hand, which healed at their touch, and finally did the same to their own. "Well, that's it. You'll need to sleep for your body to build its strength, and we'll need to get some good food in you. Soup-e maaicheh, that would be good." And relatively inexpensive, though they did not want to add money to the list of obvious worries the poor girl had. "I should be able to get lamb shanks from the market. But you're no longer sick."

Afsoneh pushed herself up. "Thank you. For every-thing." She hugged her hand to her chest. The gesture startled Firuz—it was one they used to do often as a trainee. They banished the memory as soon as it arose. "Are you sure I can stay here?" She looked from the younger sibling to the older, then back to the younger.

Parviz scratched the back of his neck, mumbled. Joints groaning, Firuz stood. "Try my cooking first before you decide."

"Avoid any eggplant," warned Parviz. "But sometimes they bring home good food."

"Again with the confidence. Thank you, Dudush."

Parviz grinned; Afsoneh giggled. Despite the pang of the joking insult—Firuz thought they were a half-decent cook—the sound made them smile as they went to get the tea.

If Firuz had been pious, they would have prayed to the godly Shahbaaz to guide Afsoneh. Maadar doted on her, teaching her Sassanian; Afsoneh picked it up with impressive ease, even though she flinched away from Maadar's affection, privately mocked the old woman's desire for closeness. Firuz had overheard the unkind comments between her and Parviz but worried interfering would injure the young teen's relationship with their brother—a relationship Afosneh threw herself into with an alarming intensity. She accompanied Parviz everywhere, ventured out on her own only if she knew where he was. When a few weeks passed and Afsoneh tentatively inquired after training, Firuz seized the chance to redirect her energies.

A month after she'd moved in, Firuz pulled closed the curtains to the clinic and blew out the lamps in the front waiting room until only a single flickering candle remained. It made sense to use this space, which was larger than the cottage and had equipment Firuz could use. As she was too young to be enrolled at the Academy, Kofi had given Firuz happy permission to train their ward here after hours; still, Firuz didn't want to risk even him walking in and learning the truth. "Now, until I find someplace better, we'll make it work here. First things first, I want to see what you can do."

"Uhm . . ." Afsoneh scratched the back of her head, swaying to unheard music. "I . . . don't know what I can do."

Firuz removed the needle in their sleeve, pricked themself hard enough for a droplet of blood to bloom on their fingertip, and held out the needle to Afsoneh after wiping it down. She did the same. "Follow my lead." They pressed their finger to hers.

Their magic rose to meet their summons, reaching towards Afsoneh's. Her own mirrored the motion, branching as Firuz's did, the threads of energy moving together like dancers. "Very good," said Firuz. "You already have a good grasp on controlling energy flow, it seems."

"I don't know what that means." Still, her magic twirled with Firuz's, running through their body, then hers, back and forth. It was an intimate relationship between any adept and teacher, and more so with blood magic. Firuz would learn the detailed rhythms of Afsoneh's magical control as their own mentor had once done theirs.

Now, they tried to remember how zhe'd once explained the core principles of magic to them long ago. "Energy is constantly flowing in the universe. It's inherent. The . . . the building blocks of our world have properties that release and consume energy. When we learn magic, we're growing the muscle, so to speak, that allows us to access this energy. Anyone can learn, but not everyone has the patience or aptitude. That's why we use the general term *magic user*, but *adept* for those who train."

Pulling away, Firuz broke the connection. They turned to the slate on the wall, picked up a piece of chalk. Drew a triangle, labeled one end. "And each of us has a school of magic we're drawn to, and each has its own sets of guiding philosophies. Environmentalists channel the forces in directions they would mostly go anyway, or else they have to balance whatever they do. So if Kofi wanted to set something on fire, something else would have to freeze—an equal and opposite reaction. You know those pots of oil and water I showed you in the rooms? Those are for Kofi to draw on as he heals." Environmental magic wasn't usually used for such detailed work, and when Firuz had watched Kofi heal in the early days of their employment, they marveled at how fine his control was.

"And what about his greenhouse?" Afsoneh interrupted. "Doesn't he grow the plants? Is that different? Can we help the others do that in the Underdock? Is that what the Academy people do on the forbidden islands?"

Firuz gestured her to slow down. "No need to rush, magelet." The teasing epithet dropped from their lips without thought; it felt apt. "Let's go out there now." They grabbed the key hanging under the front workbench that doubled as their entry table and beckoned. "As for the islands, I'm not sure. The mushrooms are central to Qilwan merchants' livelihoods, but I'd never heard of fungi the size of buildings before coming here."

"I can't believe they make boats with them," Afsoneh marveled as the two left the clinic, swinging into the alleyway housing the oven for refuse. "I wish the rest of us were allowed to go to the islands and see."

A patch of dead grass rolled into a glass house that even Afsoneh had to duck to see into after Firuz unlocked it. The greenhouse, Kofi's pride despite his innate connection to the wind, bloomed with herbs and plants and flowers that could be made into teas or tinctures or poultices or all manner of remedies. But at their feet were brown grass and dead leaves, crumbled stalks and roots.

"Plant growth is complicated magic. Like all environmental magic, it operates on the idea of equivalent change." Firuz toed the debris to the side. "To speed a plant's growth, another must give up its nutrients and energy. Grass is simple and plentiful to use as a source." Such energy exchanges, they suspected, might actually be more rooted in a plant's life force, blurring the line between environmental and blood magics as disciplines. "If the Academy scholars are doing something similar on the islands, they might not want the general public to see the cost of their merchants' trade and city's wealth."

Afsoneh knelt, ran her fingers through the detritus. "That's sad," she murmured. "Killing something so another can grow."

Kofi, were he here, would agree.

The two of them returned to the clinic after locking the greenhouse, and Firuz resumed their position at the board when Afsoneh sat back in front of it. "So, environmental magic. Equivalent exchange." Tapping another corner of the triangle, they said, "Structural magic is next. Structuralists give energy a very specific pathway to follow through runes or words. The spell must be precise to work properly. If the spell involves energetic transfer, that also has to be specified. That's how the tub at home works—it amplifies the energy a flame can give to heat the water. And I use the same idea here when I heal, using the waterwheels we have set up. Really, all magic operates on this principle, pulling energy from a source in order to manipulate it. But for us, for blood magic users, we have to pull from our own life force."

Afsoneh yawned. "So we're weaker?"

"No, we're different. All of this—it's all tapping into

the exact same energy overall. It's not different magic, just different ways of getting to the same thing." Afsoneh nodded, yawning again; Firuz barely repressed their own. The hustle of the clinic had slowed in recent weeks, but that was relative to the days of the plague. Besides, Firuz didn't know how to teach this stuff, could barely remember their own lessons. There was one thing, though, they felt was only right to explain. "The . . . brand, the one your medars had put on you. It's a structural prevention from letting you access the energy of the universe. I hear it's a painful process—"

Afsoneh's hand flew to her shoulder. She no longer looked sleepy. "I don't remember. But the mark's there." She yanked the collar of her shirt to reveal black lines spiraling downward, the edges of a tattoo near her heart. "Getting it reversed—it was like . . ." A strangled noise died in her throat as she reached to tug hair she no longer had. "It felt like I'd lost a sense I didn't even know I had. Suddenly I could feel . . . so much. Everything." She bared her throat as her head tilted up, eyes glassy and unfocused. "Especially living things. The plants in the greenhouse—I can feel them growing. I can feel your blood moving through your body. I . . ." She mouthed something, concentrating. "There are three people walking this way. I could never feel any of this before."

As she spoke, Firuz stilled. They didn't bother checking the streets; they believed her. This was a level of power Firuz did not have access to, a level they'd heard only the elders grasped. Magelet, indeed. With real training, Afsoneh could attain heights unprecedented and uncharted.

She watched them with a hopeful expression. It wasn't her fault she was stuck with Firuz as her only chance of learning enough control so as not to hurt herself or others. No, Firuz would take responsibility for her, and they'd do it properly. "Let's see if Kofi-khan has a book on basic theory to guide our lessons."

She pouted. "Homework on top of my schoolwork?"

"It's the only way you'll learn." Firuz picked up the lit candle holder and headed to the supply room in the back, where Kofi stored his reference books. They scanned the shelves. "The traditional method of training involves a lot of study before you actually practice more than basics. We don't have the luxury of time, so we'll have to do both."

But the practice aspect was not kind; Firuz's hand still ached from the memory of being broken and set too many times. The best way to learn, the elders claimed, came from working on one's own body. Maybe that was the case, but Firuz didn't know if they could abide doing the same to someone else, let alone the girl who might become their sister with time. If she stopped lashing out and let herself be loved. If Firuz had the capacity to reciprocate.

"Can I ask you something?" Afsoneh had followed them, pulling herself up onto a close-lidded barrel. "Why were my medars so afraid of my magic, if it's basically the same as any other?"

Firuz should have expected this question. Their hand plucked a book off the shelf, and they flipped through it to delay answering. "Our stories say blood magic was first taught to our people soon after our empire began. Then it was forgotten. When it returned during the Conquest—"

"The Conquest?"

Skies, the girl needed a real education. What were they teaching in that muddy school? What had she learned in whatever backwards town she'd been reared in? A backwards town that was one of the largest cities in Dilmun. "The Dilmuni Conquest of Sassanid, where the Dilmunis invaded from the sea and settled in our homeland, on command of their First Prophet of the Nameless God, and ended our empire. The stories say the science was rediscovered then, but not everyone thought it was a blessing. There was a schism—a split between those who thought it would lead to our destruction, and those who thought it could save us, since it shifted the tide of war." A schism that had Firuz and their mother constantly butting heads—she was of the opinion Firuz should abandon all blood magic forever, be only a structuralist, and Firuz was tired of arguing. "I suppose both were right."

"How come?"

"Enough Sassanians defected to the Dilmunis to stop the war, and for decades, blood magic was only practiced in secret. But now, even though it's no longer an outlawed practice, it's why we're being killed back home." There was that word again, *home*, in relation to Dilmun and not Qilwa. Firuz passed the book to Afsoneh. "Let's start with this one. We'll go through the basics and integrate some training where we can."

She took the book and pushed herself off the barrel. The sound her feet made when they hit the floor was . . . hollow. She and Firuz traded a glance before Firuz brought the candlelight closer. Afsoneh knelt, brushing off the shavings littering the floor to absorb any spills. Firuz crouched too. "You shouldn't do that without gloves."

"I'll wash my hands. Look, this one's loose." She pried up a section of the floor and squinted below. "What's down there?"

Firuz pursed their lips, considered the candle, then took off their amulet. Scratching its bottom tip against the softening wax, they carved a few simple runes to amplify the light; as brightness filled the room, they bent the candlestick into the darkness. "This might have once been used for storage."

"Spooky."

"Useful," they corrected. "If there's space down there, we might be able to use it. I should have begun with this, but you realize we have to practice in absolute secrecy, right? No one can know."

She tilted her head. "Not even Parviz?"

"No one else can know," they amended. "I'm not eager for either of us to be thrown to the governor's mercy."

For an instant, Afsoneh's face changed; her eyes

flashed, lips twisted in a snarl, a feral anger that sputtered the candle flame in its holder. Then the moment passed, the flame settled, and she nodded. "I understand."

Firuz opened their mouth to comment on her reaction, then thought better of it. "Good." They dropped the floorboard back over the hole. "I'll investigate this another time. For now, let's go home."

YEAR TWO

THE BELLS tied to the busy clinic door jangled, ringing through the chorus of complaints buzzing in the background. Firuz's hands stilled over the cracked ribs they were mending; an exhaled hiss brought their focus back. They smiled down at their patient. "I'm sorry, the door distracted me. No climbing trees for another few weeks, all right?"

"It was a request," grumbled Ahmed. "Afsoneh's fault. I don't make a habit of it."

"Afsoneh should know better than to ask people to do things she can do herself, and you should know better than to bother a bird's nest. You're lucky the parents weren't around to make matters worse."

The teen rubbed his broad nose, watching the ceiling. "She said it was for a school assignment."

"She probably wanted to see how far you'd go to impress her." Firuz removed the warm towel with the runes sewn into them and patted their patient's hand.

After trying to curl his legs towards his chest and apparently finding it uncomfortable, Ahmed sat up, wincing. "Is it supposed to still hurt?"

"The fracture is fixed, but your body still needs rest for it to fully heal." In the corner, Firuz measured broken willow bark into a cloth sack, having brought the jar over from the supplies room. "Put a cold compress on it when you get home and drink this as a tea before you go to bed. One of your mothers should be able to help you."

Had he been in a chair, Ahmed would have likely sunk into it. As it were, he cradled his head in his hands. "Nia-mama will have words, that's for sure."

Firuz hid their amusement as they tidied up, then washed their hands in the basin. They'd only met Ahmed's mothers a few times and were bad enough with names not to know one from the other, but they guessed Nia was Ahmed's no-nonsense parent, who scolded and lectured. "The next time Afsoneh tries to get you to do something ridiculous, tell her I'll double her reading."

A grin this time. "She says you give her more work than she gets at school."

Firuz's stomach lurched before they willed it to relax. They had to trust their ward had only shared that she was training—and not what she was training to become. "The price of magic is hard work, I'm afraid. Now, I have to attend to the others."

Ahmed ducked his head. "Thanks, Firuz-healer."

Firuz could tell their patients three hundred times they were only an assistant, but it would never stick. Instead, they took the offered bundle Ahmed held out—clean linens for bandages, not food; they could deal with them later—and followed him out, slipping the payment behind the front table as their patient waved goodbye. It was just them in the clinic today; Kofi had headed across the sea to go book hunting at Firuz's request.

The room was packed, as it had been nearly every day for the past two months. Most of the patients Firuz saw sustained injuries due to hard labor from working the fields or internal damage through the inhalation of rock dust from the nearby quarry, but a recent surge of different illnesses had set everyone on edge. The governor's physicker advisors hesitated to name such varied symptoms a return of the plague, as it had been over four months since the last official case, and so far, Kofi wasn't worried. Firuz didn't know what to think. When they'd last had tea with Malika, the mortician who had taken a liking to them, she'd mentioned a new influx of preserved bodies like the one she'd brought before. The news circled in Firuz's mind for days.

The political unrest with the relatively new queen in Dilmun scared enough people that an unexpected wave of migrants swept Qilwa in recent weeks—Dilmunis, too, among the Sassanians, to Firuz's interest. But since their similar features couldn't necessarily be told apart, both groups were treated the same in each other's company, and so the number of patients the clinic saw steadily increased. More patients meant less time to help Malika with the mysterious bodies, to steer her away from Firuz's people. Whoever was mucking about with the dead was still in Qilwa, and new Sassanians meant more places to hide. Or more people to blame.

In the waiting room, the drawn curtains let in the mid-afternoon sun, though the shut windows prevented a breeze. Children ran around chatting parents; an old person tended to an infant; a series of sneezes bounced around. Kofi had been considering a new locale for their work, and as owner of the officially last-standing free clinic in Qilwa, he would need to do so—and quickly—if such overload continued.

Firuz wormed through the crowd to get to a window, and a familiar face surged forward. "Assistant Healer Firuz," said the governor's clerk, eyes bright behind square spectacles, an indigo headwrap knotted above her forehead. "May you know the Nameless. Forgive my rudeness, but might I have a word?"

Firuz scowled, and not from the lack of usual pleasantries. This was the last thing Kofi—or Firuz—needed. "Look around you. Now's not a good time."

"This will not take long, please." The clerk pushed a file into Firuz's chest, sepia cheeks shining at the inadvertent contact when Firuz lifted their hands to take it. "Please get these to Healer Kofi. There's a copy of the latest law the council is considering, and we've revised our offer."

"The offer is useless." Firuz tucked the file under their arm. "But I'll tell him. If you'll excuse me." Without offering social niceties, Firuz threaded through the other patients, away from the frowning clerk, and towards the opposite wall, putting as much distance between the two of them as they could in such a packed space. So much for opening a window. They turned to the board to call for the next patient when their feet stopped and their voice caught, filling their throat so completely they almost choked.

At the door stood two boys: Ahmed, on his way out, and Parviz, bouncing on his toes as if he was about to bolt. Ahmed's head was bent towards his friend's, lips moving, before he squeezed the younger teen's shoulder and pushed open the door. Ahmed had left school early, but the tinkling laughter of children filtering in from the open door made it clear lessons were done for the day. Time always flew to the skies at the clinic.

Parviz's thumb rubbed one palm; he didn't look up as his sibling approached. They slowed their pace so the governor's clerk, still acting put out at Firuz's brusque treatment, could reach the door before them. Then, since they'd come over, Firuz leaned over a seated patient to open the window, which prompted another to do the same on the other side. With the breeze came a welcome reprieve from the stuffy room, and Firuz returned their attention to their brother, stroking his dark hair away from his sweaty, pimple-strewn forehead. "What's wrong?" They switched from the Dilmuni-accented Qilwan they usually spoke at work. "Where's Afsoneh?"

Parviz ignored the question. "I'm here to see a healer." Despite the near mumble, he looked determined as he finally lifted his chin.

Firuz motioned around them. The regulars were in conversation with their neighbors. Three children ran in circles, almost knocking over an ornate vase the governor's office had kindly "donated"—Kofi had recognized the bribe when he'd received it—before a parent finally caught one of their arms. An old person coughed into their hand. The air stank of bodies, coating the inside of Firuz's gums and their tongue. "You could have waited until I got home."

Parviz recoiled from Firuz's outstretched hand when they tried to take his. "I need to see a healer who will actually help me."

Ah, this punishment. Of course. What had they thought this was about? "Dudush, I've told you—"

"Don't. You always—always—make excuses." Parviz lifted his hands as if to cover his ears, then dropped them and gave Firuz a hard look, jaw quivering. Firuz's instincts reared to avert their gaze, to hide the red-ringed irises marking their abilities from the one person who needed those abilities—and Firuz themself—most. "I want to see Healer Kofi."

"Kofi won't be back until next week." On a personal mission for Firuz, a desperate attempt to find resources to do exactly what Parviz wanted.

One year they'd been in Qilwa, and one year Firuz

had been promising an alignment spell.

A strangled sob escaped Parviz; Firuz didn't know what to do with their hands. They wanted to hold their brother, tell him they were doing their best, that every moment not consumed by other patients or Malika's bodies or Afsoneh's training was spent working on the spell—a redistribution of the tissue on his chest to other areas, or a breakdown of that tissue for the body to repurpose; and a shifting of chemical inputs in place of the current weekly tonics. They'd switched from making the ointments, which were more time-consuming creations.

Parviz had heard this all before, of course; Firuz had been using this refrain for months. Binding could only do so much after a while, and though his hips were tolerable now, he might not think so in the future. Surgical alignments were a whole other, more invasive procedure of which Firuz had little knowledge.

Parviz lifted his elbow to hide his face. "The vest is tight, Firuz. I can't let it out anymore." His voice cracked. "I don't want them. Please don't make me keep them."

Firuz pressed their forehead to their brother's as they traced the sharp tip of their amulet. Their own alignment had happened when Parviz was a toddler, in a time and place where Firuz was unafraid of their magical affinity and went to the closest elders to train, a time where they could find other Sassanian healers to do the procedure. Qilwa was only ten years independent, and even now, despite the atrocities happening there, Dilmun still had more resources, more healers—skies, physickers too—who did alignments. Probably. Physickers who specialized in surgical alignments were hard to find. Firuz knew of only one in Qilwa, and eir prices were so astronomical, it was hard to believe ey had any patients at all. Most likely, such physical changes would still need to be augmented with future procedures to account for other alignment aspects.

All that to say: there was no one in Qilwa who could do what Parviz needed—except Firuz. Well, what Firuz would have been able to do, had they completed their training.

"Why can't you . . ." Parviz mimicked a cut across his palm, sniffing before rubbing his nose. Snot smeared on the back of his hand, and Firuz frowned at the green-yellow color. "You went through this. You know what it's like."

Firuz should have been concerned about Parviz's indiscretion, but the tears spilling to his chin stopped any potential scolding. A quick check around reminded them the clerk was gone. The others in the waiting room pointedly ignored the siblings.

"I do know what it's like." Mostly. Parviz's distress about his body had begun to ramp in recent weeks beyond what Firuz experienced pre-alignment. Cupping their brother's neck, they rubbed it soothingly to check the nodes there. Swollen. "I know it's hard. I promise I'm working on the spell. Kofi's gone back home—" Firuz's voice caught; they cleared their throat. How did they still use that word a year later?

"He's gone back to get some books for me. To help." They hoped. "You know the tea I make Maadar when she's sick? I want you to have a cup of it when you get home."

Parviz slapped his sibling's hands away before rubbing the streaks on his cheeks with his sleeve. "I'm fine. That's not what I'm here for."

A part of Firuz wanted to dispute this dismissal. Instead, they hammered themself into a calm facade. "Please. Go home and have the tea, and we can talk some more then. I need to tend to these patients."

Parviz's chin dropped to his chest before he spun around and flung open the door. For a beat, the din in the room softened, as though everyone watched the bruised boy hunched in the doorway. Then Parviz squared his shoulders and slammed the door behind him.

Were Firuz alone, they would have hidden their face in their hands. Muck bury it, but they were only one person, and they were doing their best.

They took a moment to reorient themself, step back into the headspace needed for work. Trying to push away lingering nausea from the encounter, they called and led the next two patients into different examination rooms. Their first patient—one known to Firuz from past visits—was in a good mood, which cheered them. Rotted teeth beamed as she exposed the fresh purple and older greening, yellowing bruises on her dark skin. A tiredness she could not sleep off, a weakness she did not have before. Shortness of breath, even without vigorous activity, and light-headedness. As she walked, she teetered, and Firuz noticed the overt tremor in her hands as they helped her onto the exam bed. The examination led to more confusion—clear-sounding lungs, and the lymphatic nodes in her neck and under her arms weren't swollen. But her heart palpitated, and that was a concern indeed.

They contemplated these features all together. Not an infection, so perhaps lackluster nutrition due to failing dental hygiene was the answer. Little to do for the teeth at this point, but the nutrition Firuz could help with.

"Do you know Imani on this side of the bazaar?" they asked, after returning from the supplies room with licorice root. "Ask zher to make you ghaa'oot with ginger; you can choose your favorite nuts for zher to grind. Zhe'll know what it is." The sweet powder was common in Dilmun for fatigue, and Imani, as a Sassanian of Qilwan heritage, was Firuz's go-to vendor for all foods Sassanian. "Eat it as a snack throughout the day. And make tea out of this"—they relinquished a cloth-wrapped bundle—"one stalk per cup, one cup a day, for the next week. No more than that." They sent the patient away with the instruction to return the following week if she wasn't feeling better and dismissed what they'd seen.

Until they stepped into the next exam room, where they saw almost the same symptoms. No teeth problems here, but there were again those mysterious bruises, the deep weariness; and, for this patient, a swollen, tender tongue, pink turned red. Muscle weakness was more pronounced too—where Firuz had dismissed it for their last case, chalking it up to advanced years, they could not for this middle-aged dyer. Neither was this someone with other physically strenuous responsibilities accounting for their exhaustion. In addition to what they'd prescribed earlier, they added a suggestion of grilled liver, red-meat kabobs, dates filled with walnuts. All foods meant to boost a person's energy.

Firuz wilted against the workbench, bolstering their spirits before heading back out to the rest of the crowd. Two patients didn't necessarily mean a pattern, but it was worth monitoring. And that would distract them from their brother, even for a short time.

Over the next three weeks, ten other patients came in with the symptoms of what Firuz named the blood-bruising. No amount of sleep helped; bruises would not disappear with salves or ointments, and it took an abnormally long time for any bleeding to stop. One patient came in with half their arm a rich purple so deep it was almost black, another with the yellowed eyes and skin of jaundice. None of them reported doing anything out of the ordinary, their routines mostly involving work, home, and now, the clinic.

Kofi grunted in the midst of cleaning the remnants of the day when Firuz paused while folding bandages to confront him with the evidence, flailing their meticulous report. "I've listed each patient and their symptoms," Firuz said. "Have you ever seen anything like this?"

Kofi flipped through the sheets with thumb and forefinger. Yellow-green discoloration peeked out on his wrist before it vanished from sight. "Have you read Khalaf's treatise on surgeries? He has a section on symptoms like these."

"I checked that." Firuz balanced their pendant on their thumb, fretting the sharp edge against the callus there. They'd spent hours diving into the texts in Kofi's medical library, including the handful of new books he'd brought back from his trip to Dilmun those weeks ago. The treatise Kofi mentioned was among the books Firuz had skimmed, and they'd followed that lead until it was exhausted. "From all accounts, it's hereditary. Lifelong symptoms, not developed overnight, and it only explains the slow clotting."

"Hmm." The healer stacked the pages back together, gaze turned inward, before grabbing the broom propped against the table to resume sweeping. "And the treatment, is it working? What have you tried? Maybe the humors are unbalanced." Humoral theory—the bodily relationship between blood, water, air, and bile—was Kofi's area of specialty, which, given his environmental proclivities, seemed a natural fit for him. When Kofi worked with a patient, he examined their balance of fluids, charted a thorough history to explore which behavior corroborated what result. For Kofi, balance between consumption, activity, and excretion explained many of the symptoms he saw, though he was not so archaic, he once told Firuz, to resort to such horrific devices as leeches.

Personally, Firuz thought humors were only part of how a body functioned, though they couldn't tell Kofi why they thought so. "Eating liver seems to have the most promise, but it's a temporary reprieve."

Another considered hum, another sweep. "Have you asked whether other clinics have seen cases like these?"

"Not yet." Firuz picked at a rag before forcing themself to continue folding. "Though I did run into Mazaa at the market. She said you're in the governor's bad graces again."

Kofi growled, as he always did whenever the governor was mentioned. "It's been six weeks since the latest migrants have come. Most people have placed roots here. There's no more crisis. There's no need for us to change how we treat our patients."

That wasn't entirely true; the Underdock might be home for most Sassanians, but the mold from the surrounding sea ate through their houses and bodies like rot running through saffron bulbs. And though many shops had no ethnic restrictions and plenty of Sassanians could pass besides, there were those, like Firuz's family, whose background was sketched on hooked noses and connected brows, despite these not being universal Sassanian traits, or even only Sassanian traits.

Still, Firuz gestured to themself. Too much to argue. "You don't need to tell me that. I'm proof, aren't I?" How lucky they were that Kofi hadn't batted an eye when he'd learned their ethnicity. Despite their tendency towards wariness, Firuz's defenses had slowly dissolved with Kofi's everyday affections.

Kofi's expression softened. "My wonderful Sassanian trainee. Almost a full-fledged healer." Firuz's neck heated, and Kofi clapped them on the back. "Well, why don't we—"

The clinic door opened. Firuz produced a sheet from their pile and shook it out to see the length and how many approximate bandages they might cut from the cloth.

"We're closed for . . ." Kofi trailed off.

Parviz stood inside the clinic, fists clenched, shoulders by his ears, breathing hard.

Firuz dropped the sheet. "Dudush—"

"Healer Kofi." Parviz's voice cut clear through Firuz's. "Do you have a few minutes?"

Kofi looked from one sibling to the other. Parviz's chin jutted high while Firuz tangled their hands in the linens, as if that could shield them from their brother's wrath. Kofi placed the broom against the table again. "Come to my greenhouse, Parviz-jan. Worth a harvest anyway." He shot Firuz a look they could not decipher: curiosity? Benign but present suspicion? A warning?

As Kofi left to grab a basket and shears, the silence hung like overripe fruit, ladening a branch until it sagged a tired bow. The sheet pooled at Firuz's feet as they tilted their head, tried to catch their brother's attention, but Parviz stared at the ceiling with studious interest.

When Kofi returned with his supplies, Parviz spun on his heel and marched out. Kofi did not follow, not right away. Instead, he watched Firuz.

"What?" The word came out sharper than intended.

"We did not finish our earlier conversation." A breeze twirled Kofi's coils as he twiddled his fingers. "I was going to suggest going to the other clinics together and see what they think of this blood-bruising. And, ah . . ." His hair swayed, springing back and forth. "The governor has been asking me to bring you up to her office for weeks."

Dizziness struck Firuz; they gulped air and squeezed their fists to bring themself back to focus. "She wants to meet me?"

"She is curious about you, I suppose." Kofi regarded the broom and the dirt beneath it as if by looking at it he could make it clean itself. Then he dismissed his concern, whatever it was. "And if the clinics don't turn up anything, we can consider bringing this blood-bruising to her awareness."

And risk even more legislation regulating care? Not on Firuz's watch. "Fine. You, uhm. You probably shouldn't keep him waiting." They busied themself with sweeping the last pile to avoid rubbing the stinging corners of their eyes.

A clasp on their upper arm. "Give him time," murmured Kofi. "He is young, and in pain. He does not see you as I do, stretched thin among your priorities, working harder than any I've known to save the lives of your people."

"Kofi, please—"

A squeeze. "Listen." A sliver of wind ruffled the cloud atop his head, then rushed past Firuz's. They leaned into the cool stream, which Kofi wrapped back around. "You are a good sibling, no matter what he thinks." Kofi's gentleness was almost more painful than a punch to the gut. "You do good for your communities. You are invaluable here. And you do what you can for everyone in your life. Do not despair that you cannot do everything for all. It would be impossible."

When Firuz approached Kofi over a year ago, they'd followed the rumors rustling through the streets— that the governor was trying to control the stampede of mostly Sassanian refugees, that Kofi was the only healer who would tend to the sick in exchange for food or linens or even for free. His name, whispered like a prayer, had led Firuz to his door.

Firuz never would have expected Kofi to become a source of comfort—and also one of shame for compliments they did not deserve.

They continued to stand there until Kofi let go of their arm, until the door opened and closed again. Then they turned back to the chores, shaking out the sheet they'd dropped, folding it in half, in fourths.

They shouldn't, they told themself. It was disrespecting their brother's privacy.

When they took their linens to the back, the jars of herbs and plants stood in disarray. As Firuz arranged them, they noticed some in the back, hidden and gathering dust. A single milk thistle flower lay in one jar, its magenta spines flaked off into the bottom. The stock of purslane was completely empty.

Well, they reasoned, those did need to be refilled, and Parviz had said he only needed a few minutes—surely their conversation was done by now? Plus, Kofi had mentioned a successful eucalyptus and sandalwood sapling inosculation, an experiment Firuz wanted to check, and was there a better time than now?

The door to the greenhouse lay ajar, and Firuz hovered in the shadows. If Parviz was still in there, they didn't want to—

"—deeply sympathetic, Parviz-jan, but I cannot help."

Fozooli nakon! admonished their mother's voice in their mind, despite her own proclivity for gossip. But her imagined voice was right; they should turn around, should stop before they heard more and further betrayed—

"But why?" Parviz's question was a held-back wail, the pain palpable. "I thought—you know more than Rooz, you—"

"I expect they did not tell you of my trip to Dilmun. Hold this steady for me, yes, like that. They asked me to retrieve books related to alignments."

A hush, almost whisper: "They . . . did?" Firuz's knees weakened at the surprise, the sorrow, they heard in that simple question. They were glued to the spot now, could not leave even if Parviz stormed out and saw them.

"Oh yes. I did what I could, though my resources were limited. Alignments, you know, are . . ." A shuffle, some clipping noises. "Ah, hmm. It is a difficult magic, I learned, one I do not have access to."

The ground rushed up to meet Firuz before they caught themself against the wall. Could Kofi know . . .?

"But why not?" Firuz could see their brother's silhouette, one hand at his side—maybe digging into it?—while his other supported a vine. "What's so special about it?"

In the alley, the day's moist heat adhered the thin cloth of Firuz's shirt to their back, dribbling sweat down their chest. To their ears, the chitter of afternoon birds was almost unbearably shrill. Oh, how their head hurt, their stomach a rock, their whole body flashing hot, then chilling—

"An alignment spell redistributes the tissue," began Kofi. "Turns fat to muscle, or breaks it down completely. Sometimes a surgery might supplement it, depending on the needs, or take the place of a spell entirely, if the patient is willing to undergo such methods. I am a healer, Parviz-jan, not a physicker. To attempt such a thing without the scientific knowledge or practice, rather than merely a magical one—it is unwise. I could not risk it. Only a fool goes outside when the clouds are gray."

Sassanian healers who used blood magic were taught some physicking sciences, but Firuz's knowledge . . .

Ever a coward, they escaped when Parviz sobbed.

Between the blood-bruising and Firuz's regular work, it felt nigh impossible to make time for anything else— not the alignment spell, and especially not Afsoneh's training. But Firuz needed to do something with the nervous energy growing inside them, particularly since they didn't know when Kofi wanted to visit the governor.

So at night, limiting their sleep, the eavesdropped conversation between healer and patient drove them: they buried themself again in the text with its chapter on alignment, and a few others on anatomy and puberty and magical theory, and sketched out potential spell pathways, and turned stolen afternoon hours to the subject of their ward and trainee.

Firuz started with giving her daily meditations to control her temper—which often left her reaching for her magic—and access to the energy inside her. Not even a week later, she whined she was bored, and even though the lack of patience concerned them, they moved her to doing the exercises they had done at her age. Most were designed to teach control of energy flows, like tapping into her strength to grow the length of her hair or nails, or shifting liquids from one container to the next. As expected, she mastered those within a few days and demanded more complex tasks. Firuz tried to explain, pressing the tip of their amulet into the meat of their pinky, that the purpose of the exercises was to be menial. Afsoneh hated hearing the adage of flapping one's wings before learning to fly.

"But I can do so much more," she complained at the end of the week's assignments. "If you won't let me do anything interesting, can't I try these in someone else?"

The suggestion alarmed Firuz so thoroughly they almost stopped her training entirely then and there. Instead, they calmed their agitation, cramming it into some corner of their mind to deal with later. "You could hurt someone doing that, magelet."

"I'd be careful."

"It's not up to you how they'd react. What if someone felt you rooting around and panicked? Tried to blast you out of them?"

She scoffed. They sat on one of the clinic's waiting room sofas, Firuz sorting through the clinic's most current financial reports—not great—while she performed exercises when prompted. "What if I were in someone non-magical, like Parviz?"

The stubbornness of youth! Firuz chewed the inside of their lower lip, fingers spinning the amulet again, thinking through how to stop this line of discussion.

"If something goes wrong, Parviz wouldn't be able to respond."

A pout, and then Afsoneh shot Firuz a sly look. "There's always you."

A tap-tap-tapping distracted Firuz before they realized it was their cane pen, jittering against the pages. "Fine. But only what I say and when—no acting on your own, or I might accidentally hurt you."

They doubted that would happen. What they were actually worried about was Afsoneh not being able to control herself and inadvertently killing one or both of them. They didn't think they were powerful enough to stop her, but they had no plausible excuse to give her besides *you're not ready*.

How to compel an eager, talented girl into accepting they were still fumbling with all of this—how to teach, and how to be halfway competent at it?

So Firuz began to allow Afsoneh's magic to crawl inside them, stirring their blood, changing their heart rate, even causing a firing of ticklish nerves that left them in a fit of laughter. The feeling of another shifting their body was like being back in training themself, moving energy around so they could memorize how such movement felt, the minutia of the shifts, the stutters of its trappings. "*All energy is connected,*" their mentor would say, fixated on Firuz. "*Your blood is only one way to harness it. Use it and unlock the vault of the universe. Feel it to reach out into the world. Control it, and anything energetically possible is yours.*"

Firuz had never been powerful enough to get that

far. Few blood adepts were. Most stuck to their areas of specialty; healing was especially apt, as the life energy in blood did not need to be converted to another form to be used. It was uncommon but not unheard of to use blood magic for other means—channel it into structures like runes or verbal spells, for example; turn it into heat or light. It was rare to be able to move between forms without losing much of the energy to the universe. It was invasive, unethical, and extremely tricky to use the blood of another to circumvent some of these difficulties.

Afsoneh's capabilities might reach heights of which Firuz wouldn't dare dream.

Her power, particularly without discipline, terrified them. They had no elders from which to seek counsel, no one with whom to confer. How to teach her restraint without risking her curiosity and tenacity running wild or, perhaps worse, dampening it entirely?

There was one way to teach control, whispered a part of Firuz's mind, how the elders taught all precocious adepts to rein themselves in. But Firuz had decided they wouldn't resort to the methods the elders used, which were painful and physical lessons Firuz had no desire to vicariously relive. No matter how unruly Afsoneh seemed, they promised they would not turn in that direction. Afsoneh would never have to tolerate abuses while Firuz watched. Not if they could help it.

One afternoon, while Firuz sat with their arms smeared with Afsoneh's blood, mind deliberately wandering to prevent a trained reaction to another's fiddling in their body, they found themself again returning to the issue of the blood-bruising. The incidence trickled at a steady pace, but Firuz, frustrated, was no closer to understanding it. If only they could explore the symptoms properly, allowing blood magic to do the work where structural could not. The hereditary disorder Kofi had mentioned affected clotting, thereby weakening the body as a whole, but was it also the case here? They'd already discounted the idea of it being the same, but perhaps the mechanisms were similar. After all, clotting time was increased in the blood-bruising too. How could Firuz experiment with potential cures if they couldn't comprehend the disease in the first place?

Their arm seized. Afsoneh misinterpreted their pained expression. "Like that?"

"Loosen your hold on my blood vessels." Firuz shook out their hand. "That's one way to numb the area, but you're not trying to kill it—cutting off circulation entirely can irreparably harm the tissue. Try to target the nerves instead of the vessels."

"Do they feel different?"

"Aim for the pricks of energy like lightning alongside the blood flow—that's better. Let's pause here for today."

Sweat glistened on Afsoneh's forehead. "I can keep going!"

"Maybe, but I need a break." Firuz's fingers swelled with the blood rush and returned nerve firings as

Afsoneh let go, and they flexed and massaged each digit.

When Firuz was a child, they had marveled at the innate talent some of the other trainees exhibited, their deft manipulation of the energies in their own bodies and in others', how such magic affected the world around them. For Firuz, such feats were out of their grasp. Instead, they'd found comfort in using their magic within bodies, stitching together injuries after practice, helping their village healer when accidents occurred. As an adult, Firuz no longer wished for power outside their control, and watching Afsoneh reinforced their relief at their average capabilities.

Their helplessness at what might be a new plague, however, shredded that acceptance. If they had Afsoneh's skill, then maybe they'd have more knowledge of it. If they were stronger, then maybe . . .

Then maybe they'd have been able to *create* the blood-bruising.

The thought stilled Firuz in their hand massage. Unlike the corpses dogging Mortician Malika's worries, Firuz had no evidence there was anything magical about the blood-bruising. But they'd never considered what the conditions of the preserved bodies might have been when they were still alive. Overactive blood production, however faulty, in the dead—that had to have ramifications in the living. What would manifest when a body created more blood than it needed, even if it did not have the proper ingredients available?

Blood was responsible for so much—carrying nutrients and air to organs and tissues; fighting disease and infection; clearing waste or depositing it where it could be processed for excretion. If the marrow increased its output to an unsustainable level, might that impact the type of blood produced, make it less effective at its various jobs?

Faulty blood that would not clot at a reasonable rate, leading to bruises on the skin.

Faulty blood that could not carry enough air, leading to seemingly unwarranted fatigue.

And the uneven gait many of their patients exhibited? And the pain in their lower extremities, a tingling or numbness arising whenever it pleased? And the memory loss already beginning in the earliest patients, the confusion, the visual disturbances?

"Firuz?" Afsoneh had her lower lip pinched, eyebrows furrowed. Firuz nudged her hand away from her mouth, her long nails leaving imprints. They rose and paced the clinic's waiting room, mind still pulling together any other similarities between the blood-bruising and the bodies, tendrils of connections weaving together the way injured tissue healed itself.

A strong enough blood adept could use the energy within a person's body to control its inner workings: a self-sufficient system drawing upon a life force to keep the spell going, relying on natural rhythms for its supply. A strong enough blood magic user without training wouldn't know how to deal with the implications of the spell, the eventual wear on a body until it could no longer handle the strain. Firuz didn't think they had the knowledge to plot out all the ways the spell could go awry, were they to attempt it, let alone someone who didn't know what they were doing.

Any machine, with enough use, broke down. A body was a complex machine fitting together thousands, if not millions, of parts; too much pressure on any one could cause a malfunction that collapsed the whole thing. A spell targeting blood, which reached every tissue, every organ—such a spell could do untold damage.

Such a spell was doing very specific damage.

Firuz started for the supply room. If Kofi didn't have books on the scientific processes of the body—more complex than a basic anatomy text—then they'd have to procure one. There had to be other physical characteristics they could check for in their blood-bruising patients. Too many questions lay unanswered: how contagious it was; how it began or otherwise spread; and—most importantly—whether it could be cured.

If only the Aziza Kiwabi Academy cared enough to investigate, but Firuz was afraid the scholars would pin the blood-bruising on the migrants. If this disease was a blood magic user's doing, they wouldn't technically be wrong.

"Firuz, wait!" Afsoneh's demand snapped Firuz out of their reverie; they'd forgotten she was still there. "What's going on?"

"I thought of something for work." They skimmed through the shelves, plucking up a few potential leads. Maybe Kofi's academic contacts had texts they could borrow if these didn't work.

"Oh." Afsoneh scuffed her feet against the floor. "I thought we might be going into that other space."

Firuz stacked their findings. "Other space? What other space?"

"You know." She motioned to the floor. "The one we found last year? The secret area?"

Firuz followed the course of the movement, then remembered. "Huh. I'd forgotten about it, actually. I don't know if it's a 'secret area'—it's probably old storage."

"Why is it hidden, then?" She began tapping her foot along the floor, then swept away the hay and wood shavings when she found the hollow spot. "Let's go check it out."

"It's getting late—"

Afsoneh lifted the floor panel. "Do you hear something?"

The smell of damp soil rose to meet Firuz's senses, but as they crouched, they heard it: a hiss of air, a strike of flint, the blossoming of a fire. Firuz held up a hand to stop her from coming closer. No light trickled through from the space below, though if someone was down there, Firuz didn't want Afsoneh getting hurt.

"What is it?" she whispered. "Are we going in? I think someone's down there. Oh!" She beamed. "I could check—"

"Absolutely not."

"Magically, not physically." She let the wooden door rest against Firuz before splaying her fingers. Firuz pinched the bridge of their nose. She was so stubborn, ready to dive into anything without thinking, but the chance of even another adept reacting poorly if she was only checking . . .

"Firuz-jan?"

Firuz jerked so hard the door smacked them. "Ow." They rubbed their shoulder as they peered down, a flickering candle dancing into view. " . . . Kofi?"

"So you've found the old storage space." The flame lifted, and shadows parted to reveal Kofi's hair. "I've been meaning to see what we can use this space for, but it would need quite a bit of work. Hard to breathe down here." He coughed for emphasis.

Firuz lowered the paneling to the ground. The light went out, and soon, Kofi hauled himself up and out, dusting himself off as Afsoneh dropped the door back into place. "Much better out here. I didn't realize you were training today."

"I . . . didn't know you were still at work." Firuz breathed a sigh of thanks that Kofi hadn't reappeared while Afsoneh was still practicing. Speaking of . . . Firuz's fingers flew to their opposite forearms, alarm rising in their chest at the thought of Kofi seeing the blood covering them—but they'd pulled their sleeves down out of habit at some point. Skies above, what luck.

"I lost track of time, exploring down there. Goes quite a ways. I worry the damp would eat through whatever we keep there that's not metal. And even then, the rust—"

"You're bleeding, Kofi-khan," said Afsoneh, pointing.

Kofi glanced at a cut on the inside of his forearm. "Hm? Ah, must have happened coming up. Plenty of splinters on the ladder. Hadn't even noticed." He gave Afsoneh a warm smile. "I'll clean myself up. Are you two staying long?"

"We should actually get going." Firuz picked their reading materials up from the counter before the three headed into the hallway. "Do you need help, Kofi-khan?"

"I'll be fine, they-Firuz." Kofi patted them before ducking into a room with a sink. Silly not to have one in the supply room. "Go on home. I will see you tomorrow."

Afsoneh hurried off to pack her belongings, but Firuz lingered in the doorway as Kofi cleansed his cut. Something nagged at them, though they couldn't put their finger on what. Perhaps the knowledge that Kofi was so close, while Afsoneh was in the middle of blood magic training, unnerved them. They'd thought they were being careful, but clearly not careful enough. "Kofi, did . . ." Firuz exhaled and shook their head. "Never mind."

Kofi dried his arm with gentle dabs of a towel. "Something the matter?"

"No, I was . . . ah, it's nothing." Firuz turned away. They didn't want to plant the idea they'd been doing something suspicious. Afsoneh bounded towards them, her bag slung over her shoulder. Cheerful as always. "Good night, Kofi-khan."

"Good night, Firuz-jan. Don't forget the basket in front."

"Hope it doesn't have eggplant," chirped Afsoneh. "Parviz'll throw a fit."

"No eggplant." Kofi chuckled. "It should pass his standards."

Firuz's diaphragm clenched at their brother's name—their brother, who'd been ignoring them for weeks—but they forced a smile. "Thanks. Let's go, Afsoneh."

The next week, the latest clinic-focused legislation arrived, courtesy of the governor's office. Kofi spent three-quarters of an hour ranting about the changes as he paced the clinic, Firuz watching as they sipped their tea. These early-morning or late-afternoon sessions were a common occurrence by now. "Outrageous," Kofi said, when he'd tired himself out. "I'm demanding an audience with her in two days' time."

Firuz arched a brow. "Two days?"

"Need to get her attention now, while it's on her mind." Kofi snatched up his bag. "No one from the Academy has responded to my complaints, so it is time to go to the one in charge. Close up, will you, please." The tone made it clear this was not a request. "I need to send a missive to secure the meeting."

"All right. I'll see you in the morning." They couldn't help but chuckle as Kofi continued to mutter to himself as he left, enjoying the quiet as they finished cleaning up and gathered their notes on the blood-bruising, sans their recent theory. Of course, visiting the governor was no laughing matter, and neither was Kofi's real distress, but if Firuz didn't laugh, they'd scream.

Unfortunately, when Kofi and Firuz visited the other clinics in their area two days later, their investigation turned up empty. Sure, the healers were polite enough to Firuz—some ignored Kofi, while others joked with him about resisting the governor's summons for so long—but none had seen anything like the blood-bruising. Firuz didn't think they were lying; their alarm at the description of the symptoms was real enough. Clinics on other parts of the island might have had more insights, but a few of the healers mentioned that none of their other clinician colleagues had reported such cases. Some aspect about Kofi's clinic, then, such as the number of people or its location, was related to the new disease.

That, and the possibility of a nearby blood adept.

By the time the two of them finished their interrogations, the last dregs of sunrise were fading, the day already humid. Kofi was in a foul mood after hearing the others had not been consulted regarding the newest laws, which capped the number of noncritical patients a clinic could see each day, mandated the opinion of another healer or physicker in cases of major illness, and established a minimum payment system.

"Some democracy we are," grumbled Kofi as he dragged Firuz in the opposite direction of their clinic; he'd received confirmation the day before that the governor would expect the two of them by late morning. "Let no Sassanian or Dilmuni come to us with the impression they might be allowed to take part in their own governance here. No, no, not even Qilwan citizens do anymore."

To be fair, Firuz didn't think Sassanians would be fleeing their homeland were they not forced to. A Dilmuni, though, might tire of being under a monarchy. "She can't force you to sell, right?" Firuz dabbed their forehead with their sleeve, hoping the sweat would evaporate before they arrived at the manor.

"No, but she can make it nearly impossible for us to keep open if we still want her monetary support." Kofi's grim tone, the set of his jaw, even the way his coils stirred—his nervous habit, playing with the wind—filled Firuz with queasy anxiety. "She needs to see why our work is important, what a difference we make. If we can impress upon her . . ." And Kofi gave them a pleading look, a desperate look—a hopeful one. The look of a Qilwan who'd taken a Sassanian refugee under his wing and wanted to show the results.

Oh. So that was really why Firuz was coming along.

"Besides," added Kofi, "she requested you by name."

Okay, that was strange. Firuz had never met the

governor, and being told she was asking after Kofi's assistant was different than hearing "by name."

The air sweltered as the two hurried through the streets. They'd already passed through the part of the bazaar closest to their clinic as it was opening for the day; the sellers set out bushels of lemons and oranges, teff and sorghum, imports like corn. Vendors dusted fine layers of dirt from colorful awnings; the few established buildings placed out signs enticing visitors to their doors.

Firuz and Kofi picked up breakfast from a coffee house before cutting through the neighboring residences to get to the merchant district, where houses were no longer built from brick but quarried stone from the cliffs, sitting as high as three stories. The streets here were paved, clean. No debris clogged the gutters, no animals pecked or shat wherever they pleased, and there were certainly no children huddled in tight corners, trying to ignore their hunger. The contrast to Firuz's home above the docks, let alone the slums below them, worsened their nausea.

Despite its size, there were only three mosques to the Nameless Creator on this side of the island: one at the governor's manor for city employees; one that serviced working folk in a residential district on the other side of the market from the clinic; and the final and most lavish at the edge of the merchant's quarters. Its plot began with a public courtyard, multicolored mosaics tiled around a fountain. Kofi steered them over. As if vying for attention in the central spot, a rare species of eucalyptus shot into the sky, its old bark peeled away to reveal vibrant yellow-greens and red-oranges and blue-purples underneath, a veritable rainbow of a thin trunk with faraway clusters of wiry white flowers. Other slim and less colorful eucalyptuses perfumed the air with their oblong leaves, and as Firuz inhaled the sharp scent of mint and camphor and a touch of honey, they admired the tumble of a hagenia tree's pale pink, almost orange star-shaped flowers. Only when they noticed the fiery ends of the ramrod torch lilies swaying nearby did they realize that despite the medicinal uses of these plants, all of them had been sowed for sheer enjoyment, not practicality.

Kofi fingered a lily's tubular petal, expression dark. "I can feel the growth in these," he said. "Quick. You know these did not exist two, even a year and a half ago?"

"Where's the energy source, then?" But Firuz realized the answer almost immediately. How much dead life washed up in the Underdock? Would anyone have noticed if it were dumped?

"We could use this energy to increase food production instead." Kofi left the flower for the long leaves at its base. "We could grow other medicinal plants. Trees such as these. And instead . . ." Kofi's anger, simmering for months, for longer, surged through the fountain water, arcing into the air before crashing back down. Another trickle of sweat collected on Firuz's forehead and ran into their eyes. They blinked away the salty sting.

As the water ebbed back to its babble, Kofi splashed some on his face. A couple watched him from across the meydaan, frowns marring their countenances. Firuz decided to ignore them and joined Kofi in cooling off. "It's up the hill from here, the manor." Kofi pointed a thumb at the dense foliage awaiting them in a different direction from the gilt dome of the mosque. "Drink your fill; it's a hard climb."

Firuz did not return the conversation to their mentor's earlier observation. Instead, they peered past the cultivated jungle covering the base of the governor's hill. Then their focus went up, up, up to the top, where a manor sat that put the surrounding houses and even the mosque to shame. They hadn't bothered to peer this way since they'd first arrived in Qilwa; the gleam of marble while their mother coughed at night had been too much to bear.

The two climbed in silence, following the path paved into the hillside. They frequently paused to catch their breath—and to jump out of the way of carriages that sped up alongside them, Firuz glaring in their wake—but at last they reached the gates to the building, where a row of guards stood still, their swords scabbarded or axes riding at their waists. Such guards, Firuz knew, had not existed a few years ago.

Kofi produced the governor's letter to admit them. From this high up, Firuz could see the rest of the island spill out before them: the Aziza Kiwabi Academy on the far side, with the various residential districts buffering it from the heart of the city; the farms far to the north, an attempt to offset how much food was imported; the buzzing docks, which looked almost beautiful from this vantage. From another view, might they see the mystic mushrooms on the uninhabited Qilwan islands, towering into the sky?

The gardens within also enthralled them: juniper hedges trimmed into fantastical shapes, their earthy smell filling the air; prickly white roses climbing up trellises; and right in the middle of the carriage drive-way, a magnificent acacia tree nearly the height of the manor, its leaves grouping overhead to canopy much of the walk over.

Someone with the paper-brown upturned face of a chief of staff approached them with a sniff. "Healer Kofi, you were expected half an hour ago."

"My apologies, but as you can see"—Kofi gestured—"we arrived on foot. Perhaps the governor might see fit to send a carriage next time."

"Hmm." Another sniff, then the head of house spun and strode to the entrance. "If you'll follow me, you can freshen up to make yourselves somewhat suitable before the governor."

Kofi opened his mouth, then clearly thought better of it, following up the steps in silence. Firuz surveyed their mother's handiwork, sewed for this occasion. It was no robe-like khalat, but the silk piraahan still came respectably past their knees, with stitching, around and down the open collar and wrists, reminiscent of gold zaridoozi. Firuz's mother's eyesight could not handle such fine needlepoint, but Parviz . . .

The realization gutted them.

The entranceway to the manor opened onto decor Firuz had never seen before. The high ceilings were painted with frescoes, the colors pale and pastel; columns jutted up for seemingly the sake of it, leading nowhere. The only mark of anything even somewhat Qilwan was the weighty tapestries flowing from the walls, diamond and other geometric patterns woven between triangular birds, but the creams and browns favored by Qilwan weavers—a better contrast to the colorful clothes for which the city-state was known—faded in the background against the framed landscapes hung alongside.

The chief of staff led them across padded carpets. People bowed or nodded as they passed, though each looked at Kofi and Firuz as if they did not belong—which, Firuz reasoned, they didn't.

"Is everyone here like this?" they whispered to Kofi.

He jerked a nod. "I'll never get used to it." Kofi didn't bother to keep his volume down. "Basic manners fly far across the sea, never to be found again."

To their credit, the chief of staff did not turn around. Firuz smothered their snort as the two were led into a side room.

"When you are presentable," said their guide, stiff like the so-called art behind them, "you may go into the audience chamber, down the hall and to your right. I will let the governor know you are here."

Kofi thanked them as Firuz checked their location. Even this was unnecessarily lavish—red velvet sofas, a mirror taking up the length of the wall, two golden sinks Firuz could have bathed in. There were bottles of soaps and perfumes, towels fluffier than blankets, and a rack of coats that must have been for inappropriately dressed visitors.

Both Firuz and Kofi ignored those. Firuz did not want to pander to the governor, and they supposed neither did Kofi. Kofi stripped off his own tunic and washed in the sink. "I heard the governor went on a trip south a few years ago and has since changed the decor. What say you, Firuz-jan?"

Firuz grabbed a washcloth for themself. "Uncomfortably overcompensating, which I suppose is the point."

Kofi laughed. "This is why I like you, they-Firuz. You say what's on your mind."

The two continued their impromptu bath, a hurried wash of skin and shirts, which Kofi dried with an easy wave. Their original clothes back in place, they headed towards the audience chamber. "Ready?" asked Kofi.

"As I'll ever be," said Firuz.

The dark double doors swung open, and the sniffing chief of staff—wrinkling their nose at the unchanged garments—turned to the waiting room. "Healer Kofi Nadifa and his assistant, Firuz-e Jafari."

Firuz had never head Kofi's full name before; full names weren't used often in Qilwa. "What does your mother's name mean?"

The lines around Kofi's mouth softened, but he otherwise remained impassive. "'Born between seasons.'"

"Pretty."

The audience chamber was more subdued than the entrance hall. Sure, the carpet was plush, the same dark red as the sofas in the freshening-up room, and the rich mahogany desk the governor sat at was far larger than it had any right to be, and the hung portraits of the historic queens of Qilwa were lovely, but the room was otherwise unadorned.

The governor was not alone; the city chamberlain stood beside her, straightening from the documents the two had been examining when Kofi and Firuz were announced. He was a reedy, bespectacled man whom Firuz had seen beside the governor the few times she'd come down to the city for an event. The haughty disrespect on the mustached face made their skin crawl. Off to the side cowered the clerk who'd come often to the clinic on the governor's behest, chin tucked to her chest. Her furtive glances towards Firuz as she ducked out with the chief of staff intensified their unease.

Unlike her financier, the governor was the picture of soft kindness: braided hair pulled back from her round face, a twinkle in her eye, clothes bright pink and blue and red. It seemed unimaginable that such a woman was behind the vicious laws shunting Firuz's people into extreme poverty and pain.

And then her lip curled. "Ah, Healer Kofi. You have finally graced us with your presence." No social niceties and greetings, no polite inquiries into family, not even rising—Firuz could have snarled at the clear insult.

Kofi bowed his head but did not appear dismayed

or chastised. "You must forgive me, Governor. Our clinic has been particularly busy these past months."

"So I've heard." She rose, then, swept past her companion to come around to the front of the desk. Even by Qilwan standards she was an impressive woman: tall, sturdy, and exuding an aura of confidence. Firuz had heard through the gossip of healers and patients alike that for the rich merchants of Qilwa, she was a boon and a blessing. "The pressure would lighten if you sold the clinic."

"If you have called me up for this discussion again, Governor, I'm afraid it has been a waste of both my time and yours."

"Hm. Pity." The governor's eyes flicked to Firuz. "So this is your assistant. Your patients praise your skills."

Firuz swallowed and worked to keep the wariness out of their response. "I'm glad to hear it."

"Your background," she continued, as though they had not spoken, "does not seem to bother them. Tell me, when did you and your family come here? You do have a family with you, do you not? A mother and a brother?"

The implicit threat almost raised Firuz's hackles, nearly bared their teeth like a dog. Instead, they linked their hands behind their back. "Yes, Khanoom-e Governor. We arrived about a year and a half ago."

"I see. Pray tell, what were the circumstances of your arrival?" The governor tilted her head with an innocuous blink.

"Is this line of questioning necessary, Governor?" rumbled Kofi.

Firuz shook their head. "It's all right, Kofi-khan." They flashed their most dazzling smile at the governor. "As I'm sure you know, Governor, Chamberlain, my home country of Dilmun has been under siege by both sky and land. Sky, with the ravages of the Homa bird over the last four decades; land, predominantly over the past two years, from an unknown being, group, or force specifically targeting those of Sassanian heritage. My local elders urged me to relocate my family to a place where we might be safe from both. With their permission and Kofi-khan's sponsorship, we came here."

The latter was a lie. In their gut, though, Firuz knew Kofi would let it stand.

"How interesting and unfortunate," said the governor.

"Not so," said Firuz. "We are happy here. Kofi-khan is an excellent mentor and friend." His lips crinkled at the edges, encouraging them. "I'm glad to be in Qilwa."

"This aligns with the other stories we've heard," piped in the chamberlain, whose nasally voice—seasonal hypersensitivity? masses in the sinal cavities?—made Firuz's magic itch. "Though many of your kind neglected to go through such proper channels."

Firuz felt their smile grow icy. *Your kind*, as if Qilwans and Sassanians were so fundamentally different. "Fear for one's family and own life can do that, Chamberlain. I pray you will never have to experience it."

The chamberlain sneered. "One hopes such fears turn out to be . . . unfounded."

"Unfounded?" Firuz worked their jaw up and down—would sarcasm hurt their cause?

"Assistant Healer," interrupted the governor, "you said your elders encouraged you to move here. It's my understanding most Sassanians don't have contact with their elders unless they are blood magic users."

Of course—the real reason the governor had wanted to meet them. So Qilwans were aware of modern blood magic after all, and if the open suspicion on the chamberlain's face was indicative of anything, it was the fear of such magic coming—or, perhaps, returning—to the island, where it might wreak untold havoc. And was that fear unfounded, given the preserved bodies, maybe even the blood-bruising?

"I'm afraid you've been misinformed, Governor." Even as Firuz fumed, they slowed their heart rate, forced themself to remain calm. "Many of us know the elders for other reasons. My mother is a devout woman; she only went to those elders who are priests. Further-more, I practice my healing through structural magic. Runes." They balanced their healer's bag on their hip. From behind them came a shift of leather and metal. Firuz gave the suspicious guards a cool look, despite the bulge of nerves in their throat at the unsheathed weapons, before extracting a brush and bottle of ink to show. "Only when necessary, of course. Most patients can be treated with physicking sciences rather than magical ones."

"Governor." Kofi sounded wearier than Firuz had ever heard him. "Did you call us here to interrogate my assistant, or did you want to discuss your latest legislation?"

The governor's focus stayed on Firuz for too long before she turned to Kofi. "I believe it was you who has grievances against it, Healer Kofi. Unfortunately, Physicker Faizah could not join us today, but we designed these plans together with her full support." If Kofi twitched upon hearing the name of an old university colleague, Firuz didn't see. "Tell me your objections, and perhaps we can sort something out."

Pitfalls in every suggestion. Firuz forced themself to breathe as Kofi launched into his diatribe against a patient quota, a minimum payment, a mandatory second opinion. As patrons of the sole free clinic left standing, Kofi's patients could not afford these changes.

The governor folded her hands in her lap. "The council passed these bills unanimously, Kofi. It's how clinics that receive our funding can continue to function."

"The city coffers are, unfortunately, not so full that we can be as generous as we would like," added the chamberlain.

The lie was so foul, Firuz could smell it from the slums.

"I am sorry to hear you say that, Chamberlain." Kofi picked up his healer bag with a nonchalance Firuz hoped to emulate. "I believe you will find the treasury a little fuller from here on out."

The chamberlain's pinched visage curdled the remnants of attempted compromise in the air. "And why is that, Healer?"

"Because if this is what needs to happen to be funded by the government, then I will no longer take such money." Kofi nodded. "Good day Governor, Chamberlain. Come, Firuz. Our patients await."

Finally. Kofi had been debating this decision for weeks, and it was about time he'd made it. This would make the day-to-day of running the clinic difficult moving forward, but not impossible. Firuz gripped their bag tighter. Forward was where they were headed.

"You always did love Sassanians more than your fellow Qilwans," said the governor. Kofi stiffened. Firuz gaped. Kofi's partner had died over a decade ago, but the comment was still unkind, to say the least. "Should you change your mind," she continued, "you know where to find me."

Kofi did not bother to respond.

A mere week after the disastrous visit to the governor's office, a few dozen migrants arrived at Qilwa's shores, claiming to be the last group of Sassanians left in Dilmun. A shuffle ensued: the Underdock, ever bloated, spilled into the nearby shore at the edge of the long-established quarry, which provided many Sassanians their meager-paying jobs and most wealthy Qilwans their building materials. But the arrival of the newcomers demanded a citizen demonstration, despite the need for bodies to mine rock or work the limited farms, and as Firuz bandaged those who'd been caught amid the protest, their mind wandered. The last group of Sassanians, as though whatever hunting them had completed its task. The migrants who came through the clinic, new and established alike, vibrated with this possibility, their anxious whispers dismayed at the Dilmuni queen's inaction, wondering whether the whole thing had been orchestrated by her new government.

Firuz didn't have time to ruminate. The influx of people and almost-riot were on top of the rising incidence of blood-bruising, which was either highly contagious or its creator highly active. As before, Firuz spent many nights in the clinic, not so much for waiting patients but because it became easier than going home. That, and it was the only time where Firuz and Kofi could discuss business. Staying at the clinic also helped Firuz cut back on food; if they were home, their family would undoubtedly have noticed they were trying to stretch each meal, in case Kofi could no longer pay their scant salary.

Two weeks after the migrants arrived, Afsoneh ambushed Firuz as the day was winding down. Her training had taken less priority recently, and it was only after clinic hours, when Firuz was alone, that she could grab some time with them.

The two spent the early evening going over what she'd been reading, practicing the techniques described in the book. Squinting at the page, eyes aching, Firuz rose to light a candle and realized how late it was. "We should go home," they said. Afsoneh yawned. "Yes, precisely. C'mon, grab your things."

Afsoneh faked shock. "You're actually coming home tonight? Have you been avoiding us, Rooz?"

The nickname made their chest ache. "No, Afsoneh-jan." Firuz kissed the top of her hair. It had grown in soft curls past her shoulders, the color tinged reddish from the sun. Only Parviz used to warrant such natural affection. "It's been easier to stay here, with all this work. Yes, I'll come home tonight."

After locking up, the two trudged down the darkened street. Despite the cottage sitting above the Underdock, getting home still required walking through the place Firuz and their family had once lived. Firuz hated it. No matter how many patients they treated, walking through the slums reminded them of all the people they'd left behind.

Though it wasn't too late, darkness usually urged people off the streets. In the early days, the Underdock had teemed with crowds at all hours. The encampments had given way to run-down shacks, and aside from the recent hullabaloo, the area had established an uneasy peace with the rest of the city. The guard was not called for local disputes—some people had tried, with painful results—but neither did it raid the area like it once had. Indeed, governmental officials could be seen every few weeks cleaning up garbage and handing out food, as though that was enough.

But now, with more unexpected migrants cresting the waves, familiar fears returned: the plague, the plague, the plague.

Fog was rolling in, which was not uncommon, but to see such empty streets before it had fully descended was disquieting. The planks of wood serving as doors were shut, curtains drawn, and only a few had already placed fog-catchers for water. Firuz heaved a deep sigh. Afsoneh tugged on their sleeve, cocked her head. Firuz nodded. Somewhere nearby, a migrant had been—or was currently being—targeted.

They shouldn't have been surprised anti-migrant sentiment had reemerged. One of the reasons they'd been so desperate to move their family, besides the squalid living conditions, was to avoid the violence enacted on their people as much as possible. Firuz had collected the names of local property owners, but no one outside the docks had answered their knocks. Fortunately, the location of their home, despite being in the same overall district, was removed enough from the worst of what happened in the slums. The quiet rhythm of being Sassanian in Qilwa had seemed to settle in recently. Too soon, apparently.

Their muscles ached and their temples throbbed from their long hours, but still Firuz pressed their thumb into the needle in their sleeve as they took the lead. They were not a powerful enough adept to feel the ebb and shift of heated blood, but the echoes of fighting would reach them soon enough. They knew that from experience.

Indecipherable taunts, evident from the tonal inflection, drifted towards both of them as they ducked around corners and minded alleyways. Finally, tucked between two of the only erected buildings in the area, stood a handful of individuals laughing at something on the ground.

Afsoneh lifted her thumb to her mouth to gnaw on the nail. "I recognize those kids. I think they go to the school near ours." The real school, then, unlike the one to which the migrant kids were relegated.

"I'm impressed you can tell who they are from here." Firuz didn't have great faraway vision—actually, they really should save for lenses—and with the addition of the thickening haze, they strained to see how many kids there were. "Stay here, then. I don't want to give them a reason to target you next time." What was on the ground they could not tell either, though they hoped it wasn't a person.

Afsoneh watched the group with wary distrust. Then her eyes widened. "Oh—oh, mud—"

"Hm?" In the dark, the fog bunching towards their knees, Firuz still only saw vague shapes. "What is— Afsoneh, wait!"

She pelted down the alley, shouting at the group. Firuz ran after her on instinct. As they drew closer, the figures became clearer, as did their target on the ground.

Huh, Parviz had been working on a shirt that red. And the bag tossed nearby, he used a sack like that for school . . .

With growing horror, Firuz's footsteps slowed, recognition freezing them in place. No. Not their brother, mist curling around his crumpled form. Not Parviz.

Their blood roared into their throat, lips twisting in a snarl as they tore their sleeve-needle into their palm and lifted their hands.

But Afsoneh had gotten there first. She slid to Parviz's side, rubbed his face for his blood, and surged up to slap one of the bullies. The other reared, but before anyone could react further at this firebrand in their midst, Afsoneh picked up a rock from the ground and smashed it into her hand. She hadn't even bothered to draw her own blood first.

The marked bully howled, holding up a hand—a clearly broken one, already swollen and three of the fingers bent at a wrong angle. Firuz certainly hadn't trained Afsoneh on working with another's blood; how could they, without knowing the method themself? That level of power scared them, kept them unmoving.

Who was this child they'd taken in?

Several of the kids scattered at the demonstration, squealing about cursed magics. They barreled past Firuz, not even bothering to look at them. The others cowered, slipping in their hurry to back away. The fog oozed around them.

"Never come near him again, do you hear me?" Afsoneh pulled on her fingers, and her puppet howled, clutching their hand. Most of the rest turned wing and bolted down the alley. One of the remaining kids yanked on the injured one's sleeve. They didn't need to be told twice and fled too.

Afsoneh and Parviz's huddled forms were little more than vague shapes, so Firuz circled around them, shuffling stones to create a perimeter, murmuring names of runes in an attempt to clear the spot. The Shahbaaz must have smiled on the disbelieving child of Ous disciple because it worked.

Afsoneh pushed the garbage on the street away from Parviz as he whimpered, taking care not to touch his injuries, chittering nonsense about taking care of him. But she was obviously aware of Firuz's lumbering steps, her back stiff as they approached.

Firuz almost—almost—grabbed and shook her, almost shrieked at her careless demonstration of blood magic in a place that already hated their people for cramming the streets. Someone who intimately knew this, the memory of her parents' death during a food riot still waking her at night. Someone who crawled into Firuz's cot after those nightmares and cried into their shirt until she fell back asleep. After the governor's warning, Firuz knew they had to be even more careful, even more diligent, not to give her further reason to hate their people.

Afsoneh met Firuz's enflamed gaze with cool nonchalance—except there were other emotions under it. Despite her defiance, bags sank her eyes in her skull, the purple-brown marring her olive skin. Her shoulders drooped, as if her show of magic had exhausted her. The back of Firuz's neck prickled. A long cut inched out from under Afsoneh's collar. There were scratches on the back of her hand. She was pale, peaky, and her breaths came in fluttering stutters.

Parviz groaned below them, and Firuz dropped to his side, thoughts scattering like coconut seeds bobbing on the Qilwan sea.

"Dudush . . ." Firuz cradled Parviz's head. His nose was broken, his gums bloody, and one eye was swollen shut. Even Afsoneh looked scared, bending down to take his hand. Firuz bit, hard, the inside of their lower lip to stem frustrated tears and instead sniffed and exhaled. "You're going to be okay. Try to stay calm."

Fortunately, the damage was easy to heal, mostly superficial. Firuz smoothed Parviz's thick eyebrows, using his dried blood and their own on their palms as an entry point into his body. They soothed the inflammation around the black eye, straightened and healed his angled Sassanian nose—that took a bit of finesse, since blood did not dwell in cartilage the way it did other tissue—stitched the skin in and around his mouth. No broken ribs, only bruises, and when Firuz was done, they wiped their sweaty brow. Their spell kept the area clear, but the fog roiled around them, waiting.

Afsoneh helped Parviz sit up. He touched his chest gingerly and pressed a hand to his cheek. "You fixed me?"

"You'll need to wash up before Maadar sees you

and forces you to prayer," was Firuz's reply as they disrupted the circle of stones. Afsoneh grimaced; while she had warmed considerably to the old woman, she, like the other two, dodged prayer whenever possible. "Come along, bacheha."

The walk home was quiet. Afsoneh supported Parviz, and Firuz pondered the private talk they would have to have with her. Their temper had cooled into a tired flame, like embers from the ceremonial Chahaarshanbeh Soori fire before Norooz. Their muscles ached with the coiled energy they'd summoned. Parviz was not the only one who could use a bath right now, but a bathhouse was out of the question. Chances were too high of their mother being there.

The house was empty when they arrived. While Parviz readied his bath, Afsoneh raided the pantry, and Firuz leaned against a post, arms crossed. "We need to talk."

Afsoneh crammed a pentagon-shaped dolmeh into her mouth. "Can we have this conversation another time?" It came out muffled as she chewed.

"No." Firuz grabbed her arm as she made to pass them, then took both her hands in theirs. "Listen to me. What you did was careless."

She fidgeted but did not tug away. "I knew what I was doing."

Stubborn child. Firuz traced the scratches around her wrists. "No, you didn't. You were scared and acted. It's okay, it happens. The problem is, it can't happen here in Qilwa." Firuz knew the kind of temper Afsoneh had—she had no problem turning it on them during training—but they'd hoped regular meditation would have contained her impulse to reach immediately for her magic. Of course, using the tools of control in a calm situation required less willpower than reaching for them in the heat of the moment.

The scratches peeled open; blood pooled on her palm lines. Nonplussed, Firuz watched as she aggregated the available fluid into a single drop, rolling it from her hand to theirs. She shouldn't have the focus to reopen a cut. "Why does this keep happening, Firuz?" she whispered. "Why do they hate us so much?"

"Everyone's afraid of another plague." Firuz turned Afsoneh's wrist over. The lines there were raised, the pink of recent healing. Not scars, and not from their training. "Do you know why your family left Dilmun?"

Agitation rolled off her. Firuz knew the question summoned unwanted memories. "Sassanians were being killed."

Firuz had not recounted to the governor the extent of how terrifying it had been in Dilmun. The perils of the monstrous Homa bird had become everyday—the old queen had rallied hope in the people that, at last, she would be able to ground the skyborne hazard. But after her death on the battlefield, the fear of a Homa attack had morphed into a nostalgic desire. At least the Homa was visible when it left its roost, its shadow a clear indication of impending carnage. Not so with the targeted and skillful slaughter of Sassanians that had begun afterward. First with missing people, then with whole neighborhoods wiped out. With Rahaa Village disappearing overnight. Anyone in contact with the elders became targets, and Sassanians who could pass as Dilmuni or Qilwan or any other ethnicity relocated to those neighborhoods in the cities. What else could the remaining people do but flee, terrified they would be next? Dilmun might have been the Sassanian ancestral home, but that was not enough reason to stay in light of a genocide.

Firuz let go of Afsoneh's hands and licked the single drop of blood on their palm. Not their preferred method for access, but it allowed them to slip magical awareness along Afsoneh's skin, rummaging around for other recently healed tissue. "Do you know why?"

"We were hunted? No." She wriggled and grabbed a plate, as though her worry a moment ago was forgotten. "That tickles. What are you looking for?"

"Can you pinpoint where I am?"

"My collarbone. Now between my shoulders." Deft fingers snatched taaftoon bread and soft sheep's cheese, a handful of nuts, and half an already split pomegranate. "My lower back. Left leg. Pinky toe."

"Huh." They released their hold on her. Yes, there was some inflammation around her ankles and a raised line running from her collarbone to her hip. "You're improving."

"I'm a quick learner." She blinked over at them, all innocence, as she headed down the hall to the bedroom she shared with Firuz and Parviz. It was cramped with the three of them, but Firuz spent half their nights at the clinic anyway. "Are you going to tell me why you're asking these questions?"

As they followed her, Firuz ticked through the options of where to take this conversation, how to impart their anxieties without cowing her or erasing the things that made this young teen who she was. "Do you know why I stopped my healer training early?"

Pondering this, she toyed with a walnut. "The same reason the rest of us needed to flee?"

"No." Memories surged through their mind: the long nights puzzling through structural theory; their mother stomping her foot, demanding to die on the same land as her husband; Parviz crying when he heard they needed to leave, after their mother had been convinced. "This was still in the relative early days, when those were only rumors. My—our elders told me to start training as a structural magic user, in case I would have to hide my affinity for blood."

"Why?" The plate tilted the longer she stood. Firuz plucked the pomegranate as they walked past her and into the room, which alerted her to the tipping surface. She placed it on the dresser inside but remained standing.

Firuz peeled the white layer back to reveal the crimson seeds. Tart and delicious. "The elders worried blood adepts were specifically in danger of being targeted." Had they been right? How many dead Sassanians had known the sacred science and perished because of it? Firuz might never know. "If the people tasked with keeping our community safe suspected it, I trust their judgment. That's why I had to stop training and learn structural theory. That's why it's important not to reveal ourselves, with Dilmun only a day's sail away."

Afsoneh folded her thumb and forefinger around her wrist; her index covered her thumbnail completely. Firuz added it to the growing list of what they hoped was only Afsoneh practicing in secret and not something else. "I understand." Her voice was quiet, unhappy, but Firuz heard a tinge of resignation and—more importantly—true realization as to the weight of their words. Perhaps the implicit risk was enough to caution her towards the restraint she'd been lacking.

Still, it didn't hurt to be sure. "Do you promise"—they stressed the word—"to never be careless with magic again?"

She didn't meet their eyes but nodded. "I promise."

They rubbed the veins bulging on their forehead. "All right. I hope we don't need to repeat this conversation."

Parviz walked in then, clutching a towel around himself. "I need to change." There were bruises on his back, his chest, yellow and green marks on his arms, bronze skin turned purple. Too many of them were faded to all be from the assault.

Afsoneh ducked out, but Firuz lingered. Parviz's unamused expression followed them. "You can go now."

Despite this, Firuz's feet took them forward, not back, and they tried to keep panic at bay as they traced the finger-shaped marks on Parviz's shoulders. "What's this? What happened?"

Parviz jerked out of their reach as he got a loose nightshirt. "I was attacked like an hour ago. What do you think? Turn around so I can change."

Firuz obeyed. "These are older. Let me take a look."

"I'm fine."

The two had been speaking less and less, and after their argument at the clinic—when was that, already three, four months ago? Firuz never mentioned the overheard conversation in the greenhouse either— Parviz had treated Firuz like a ghost. And Firuz understood; truly, they did. Puberty had taken them unawares, not because they did not know it would happen but because their body began to morph into a thing unknown, a thing untenable with their own image of themself, an image they hadn't realized they'd held so firmly. So they'd procured the binding vest and marched to the elders, beginning alignment processes as soon as they could. Having a set of people who could help Firuz live as the person they wanted to had made all the difference, and it was fear stopping Firuz from being what those people had been to them for their brother now.

There were so many what-ifs. What if the spell Firuz was working on, in their very limited spare time, backfired, hurt Parviz in some irreversible way? Or worse, killed him? Alignments were tricky things: mobilizing the body's systems, the process broke down unwanted tissue and redistributed the elements elsewhere. What if a clot became lodged in an organ or artery and stopped blood flow entirely? What if the shifting caused internal bleeding? What if the modulation of internal signals caused a cascade of other unintended effects? Firuz wouldn't be able to live with themself if they didn't try everything they could to make sure the spell was as safe as possible. Since Parviz wasn't a magic user himself, he didn't appreciate the ramifications and risks, and Firuz was doing a poor job impressing them upon him.

"Has Afsoneh been practicing on you?" The words were out before they could catch them. They winced, but it was too late.

Parviz whirled around, hand coming up to stab his index finger in his sibling's chest. "What is your problem? I saw her face—what did you say to her this time? Aren't you too busy with work to care about your family, let alone a random kid you picked up off the streets?"

The blow landed exactly where he'd no doubt planned. Firuz swallowed back the torrential guilt before it could choke them, before it could burst the pockets of air in their lungs and consume them. Firuz really had neglected their mother and brother, but it was to build them a good life here. That meant working too many hours for too little pay, collapsing on their cot or the living room sofa when—or if—they got home, and getting up before Parviz and Afsoneh left for school to prepare for the family's day. Firuz could get angry, could yell about Parviz's youth barring him from reality, but it wasn't his fault. The problem was, Firuz wasn't sure if it was entirely their fault either.

They turned towards the door as Parviz jammed on the rest of his clothes, but paused to look back at their brother. Parviz pointedly ignored them by surveying himself in the mirror, grabbing a comb to run through his thick curls—Firuz's coarse hair was straight; Parviz had gotten their mother's—before grimacing and prodding the red bumps on the edge of his nose. Firuz fingered their own hook, remembering the times they'd popped their pimples instead of letting them be.

"What?" snapped Parviz, pulling back from his reflection and stomping to the door. "Stop looking at me like that. Bad enough most of the leftovers are eggplant."

In the silence of the room after Parviz's departure, for the first time in what might have been years, Firuz leaned against the wall and, wondering how they'd manage to go into work tomorrow, began to cry.

Firuz folded the white burial cloth around the third patient of theirs that had, that week alone, arrived at Malika's mortuary. This one particularly hurt; the child was only six. "It's this new disease I'm seeing," they said quietly, fingers curled around the fabric. "I've been calling it the blood-bruising. I think it's related to the preserved bodies."

Malika lowered her mask to hang around her neck. "Oh?"

Muck. Firuz was so tired of hiding their magical affinity. "I don't know for sure"—and they didn't—"but it seems too much coincidence that it picks up force and you still have these bodies."

"I can keep this one around, see if it follows the patterns."

"No." Firuz pulled off their gloves and threw them in the waste bucket. "It's not worth the families having to wait. Burning the bodies is already bad enough. Besides, at the rate this is spreading, you won't have the space."

Malika motioned to the door to her sitting room. "Let's have some tea. Tell me about this disease. What did you call it?"

They repeated the name, following, then washed their hands as Malika readied some tea. They sunk onto the couch and stared up at the ceiling until she returned with a tray. "Since we talked with the governor—"

"Muck bury her."

"—we've had forty-one patients come through with the symptoms. That was . . . ah, six weeks ago, I think."

Malika poured out the first cup, returned it to the pot, and poured out another, darker glassful. She put the glass on a saucer and placed it in front of Firuz. "And the symptoms are?"

"Bruises, constant exhaustion, slow blood clotting. In some of the worse cases, memory loss and gait abnormalities too." Firuz reached for their tea, shaking themself awake. "Only recently has it started killing people. Muck, I should check on the other patients."

"You're exhausted." Malika put a plate of dates and cookies in front of them. "Eat. You need a day off."

"I can't afford to take a day off." Firuz picked up a ma'amoul and bit into it, the date filling warming them with unexpected homesickness. A variation of the cookie filled with walnut paste was common at Sassanian gatherings. "Not that my family hasn't been saying the same thing. Did I tell you Parviz was assaulted a couple weeks ago?"

"What?" Malika put down her tea, alarmed. "No, you did not! What happened?"

As Firuz recounted the story—conveniently neglecting the blood magic they had almost done and the blood magic Afsoneh had—Malika's expression became graver, more distressed. "Muck, I'm sorry. How's he doing now?"

"Well, he still barely talks to me, but he seems okay." Firuz knew they could excuse themself to splash water on their face, place a cold cloth against their neck to wake themself up, but instead, they accepted another cookie from the plate Malika now held out. "Afsoneh hasn't said anything, and I think she would if something serious was happening."

"How's her training going?"

"Slow. I never—"

"Have time, of course not." Malika clasped Firuz's wrist and squeezed before letting go. "I can't help in that department, but I'm always willing to lend an ear."

Firuz smiled. It was so nice someone around their age—Malika was only a few years older—to talk with, even if they couldn't be entirely honest. They'd never really had a good friend before. "Thanks. Same goes to you. How are your parents doing?"

The two were immersed in conversation, Firuz actually relaxing, when the door to the mortuary opened. Afsoneh peeked in. "Malika-khan, have you seen—oh! You are here, after all."

Malika didn't bother to keep a water clock—"The dead don't arrive on a schedule, Firuz"—so Firuz had no idea what time it was. The sun was still bright outside, with no signs of setting. Was it after lessons already? "Did you need me?"

"If you're free . . ." Afsoneh noticed the tea and cookies. "Ooh, are those kooloocheh?"

Firuz patted the seat beside them. "Close enough. Take a seat for a bit, and then we'll go out for some practice. How does that sound?"

Afsoneh beamed.

True to their word, Firuz and Afsoneh left after she'd had her own cup of tea. The mortuary was down the street from the bookshop school, the other side of the bazaar from the clinic. Afsoneh bounced on her toes, half dancing.

"Observational only," they said. "Let's stretch your range today."

The market was still open. Firuz slid one hand in their pocket, the other clutching their bag, and strolled along, pausing to stop at this stall and that. As they greeted the sellers they knew, Afsoneh hovered behind them, eyes moving to take in invisible streams of energy. People bustled through the street: families shopping for the evening meal, children picking up a snack after lessons, friends deciding which tea or coffee house to peruse. Two workers carried a long piece of wood through the crowd; Afsoneh ducked under it, narrowly dodging someone who did the same. Firuz took her wrist, navigating them both as bodies brushed by. Her blood reacted to their touch, and they nudged the energy out beyond the two of them. This kind of practice, with Firuz on Afsoneh's energetic tail as she stretched into the world, was safe enough, even in public. It gave her a touchstone, a way to ground herself in the chaos around her, with Firuz monitoring.

"I'm surprised Kofi didn't open the clinic today," she said as they wound their way to the edge of the district.

"We had a backlog of work and too many bodies." Firuz didn't mean to sound so grim. "I'd like to check on a patient before we go home, though. Your friend Ahmed."

She frowned. "Did he hurt his ribs doing something silly again?"

Firuz chuckled. Leave it to Afsoneh to pretend like she'd had nothing to do with that specific encounter. "No, but last I saw him, he said he'd been more tired than usual, so I want to make sure he's all right." Make sure he was out of danger, more like.

The two emerged into the quiet neighborhood that housed the clinic at its edge. A pair of dogs chased each other down the dirt road. From somewhere nearby, a baby cried. Trees fanned around them, the leaves bright green, some almost yellow, though the shade did not help the sweat trickling down Firuz's neck. Then down another street, this one with more people—way more people. Too many people.

A dozen or so gathered in front of a house, murmuring as a sharp wail tore from inside. Firuz and Afsoneh glanced at each other before hurrying towards the group. Firuz's mouth dried the closer they came, and they gripped their amulet. It wasn't a random house—it was where Firuz was headed. Any sleepiness they'd felt earlier fled.

"It's Firuz-healer!" someone called. In another circumstance, the inappropriate title would have fondly exasperated them.

Amid a chorus of relieved cries and their own confusion, Firuz was hustled forward. Once at the front, they turned to face the group. "What's going on?"

"We don't know!"

"We heard screams—"

"She who conceals her disease cannot expect to be cured—"

"It's Ahmed," murmured someone beside them. "He's gotten worse."

Muck. They searched for their ward and spotted her shoving her way towards them. Once she halted, they grabbed her. "You know where Kofi lives, right? Go get him as quick as you can." She squeezed and released their hand, worming her way back through the crowd before dashing down the street.

With firm instructions for everyone else to wait outside, Firuz pushed open the door and stepped inside the house. "Excuse me, khanoomha, are you in? It's Firuz, from the clinic."

"Firuz-healer!" One of Ahmed's mothers stumbled out from the back, which made them uneasy. Firuz, ever awful with names, could only identify her as the sweet or gentle mother, the softer one who was willing to overlook Ahmed's antics. Her skin, usually sun-darkened, was ashen, hands shaking as she reached to grasp Firuz's. "Our prayers have been answered. Come, come, please, can't you do anything for him?"

They followed the dragging blue of her chaador—they didn't know the Qilwan word for the head-to-toe drapery—into the farthest room, where Ahmed's other mother, the no-nonsense one, rocked back and forth next to the bed.

The gangly teen was so white he was chalky, his skin stretched tight over the bones of his face, sweat glistening on his brow. His breath rattled through flaking, cracked lips, his eyes open and glassy. The gentle mother took a cloth from a basin of water and dabbed her son's forehead, standing so as not to obstruct Firuz's view.

Firuz shifted their sleeve so the needle could press into their thumb. Maybe resorting to blood magic right now was risky at best and unethical at worst, but they'd seen Ahmed only a week ago, laughing with Afsoneh and Parviz. This house call was supposed to dismiss the blood-bruising, not confirm it.

They had not expected a dying teen.

Firuz sat on the edge of the bed, pulling from their bag the funnel that amplified the heart's beat. They hid the smear of their blood on Ahmed's too-hot skin and, as they pressed their ear against the funnel, sent their magic deep into his veins.

A fever was boiling him alive. His bone marrow was in overdrive, pumping out new blood at an alarming rate, thinning the bone itself to do so. But its creation was wrong and would result in a dysfunctional product, and as Firuz followed its path through Ahmed's body, they found other disturbing traits—an enlarged spleen, designed to destroy flawed or old blood; his heart, pumping so fast and irregularly Firuz had to slow their own to make sure there wasn't some sort of synergistic effect. There was not enough air reaching each organ, and the blood vessels themselves were inflamed, and maybe there was something to Kofi's theory that this was a humoral imbalance.

But oh, there was more—if this was the blood-bruising, which Firuz had little doubt it was, then it had morphed. Because the blood-bruising as Firuz had known it did not destroy the blood's capacity to fight infection, yet the disease here had its sights set on devouring Ahmed from the inside out.

He coughed. Red flew from his mouth, splattering

his shirtfront. Firuz shoved their magic deeper, hunting for the root of the infection—it might not be the cause, but it certainly was a symptom. They reached for their bag, groping without looking. When they touched supple leather, they focused long enough to draw out a bottle of ink and brush before turning back to their patient and lifting his sweat-soaked shirt.

Bruises covered his chest. On his dark skin, the healing ones colored the area a pale green-yellow, popping remaining blood vessels to the surface—not the usual blue or red but a pulsing purple, blending into any fresh marks, like ripping open a pomegranate to see rotted seeds mixed with fresh ones. More worried than baffled, as they did not want to think about the implications of a morphed and mutated disease, Firuz dipped the brush into the inkwell, went to write runes on Ahmed's chest—and then a bruise materialized where the soft bristles pressed.

And then another. And another.

Firuz shoved the writing supplies away to grab the scalpel waiting in their bag. They distantly heard sobs in the background; they had no choice, had to do whatever it took to save the boy, secrets be mucked. With a steady and light motion, Firuz sliced into the middle of Ahmed's torso, opened the heel of their palm, and pressed their hand down.

Buzzing, angry magic surged from inside Ahmed's veins, a snake striking at Firuz. Their hold stumbled, but they pushed back on the intrusion, energetically wrapping around and strangling it. It didn't feel like any parasite Firuz knew, but it moved like one, reaching out for any life to sink claws into. *Magic is mostly a working of the will*, Firuz's old mentor used to say, and Firuz used that now—refused to submit to the invading presence, held their grip in place as they pushed further into the heart of the interloper. Some mobilization of the blood, the healer in them documented—this metaphorical and yet tangible leech was not endemic to Ahmed's body and yet here it was, a part of him, a part rearing with the energy of unchecked and unsustainable blood creation, tainted and hungry for satiation.

So when Firuz opened themself up and invited the invader in, it slithered inside, ready to consume.

But blood magic training had ensured airtight control over their body's rhythms. Firuz's magic smothered the sickness and yanked it out like a weed in the greenhouse, and it sizzled before dissipating, before Firuz's own body took stock of the parasitic elements and decided such blood would be a poison, and sequestered it for later destruction.

Someone screamed. Firuz opened their eyes—when had they closed?—and gaped at the scene before them.

Blood had poured from Ahmed's eyes, pooling in the hollows of his cheeks. His lips were bright red and drawn back from his gums, tongue lolling to the side, teeth bared in a frozen grin. Firuz had left a red handprint on his torso, and the place they'd cut was splayed open several fingers' width. Yet Ahmed was still, somehow, alive; his chest heaved, short gasps expelling a cloying sweetness into the air, coating Firuz's mouth and throat.

"But how . . ." Firuz trailed off as they took stock of themself. Their hands were red enough to look hennaed. Their shirt clung wetly to them; blood had seeped through as if they'd been the one cut. They touched the cloth, far away from their body, from this moment.

A thin red bubble bloomed on Ahmed's chest, ballooning like a bladder. "My son!" wailed one mother, breaking away from her stunned, oft-gentle wife. "What's happening to my son!"

The bubble burst before she reached them, showering the room in blood. Firuz spluttered, spitting out the metallic tang. Ahmed's mother didn't pause; she pushed them aside and slid on the bed to cradle her child. Ahmed's milky yellow eyes turned to her, and that grin, that skin-pulled-back, too painfully tight grin, seemed to broaden. He took one last shuddering breath, then stilled.

"Drink." Kofi pressed a warm cup into Firuz's grasp. "It'll help."

Firuz automatically lifted the drink. The soothing smell of mint wafted up; their tongue tasted menthol and honey. "I thought I had it, Kofi. I thought I was going to save him."

Kofi perched beside them. "It's not your fault. This happens. Sometimes there's nothing you can do."

Firuz didn't know how long they'd been sitting on the clinic sofa after Kofi had guided them back. They'd stared at the body as chaos swirled around them. Whether Ahmed's mothers had been screaming at them or just in general was unclear; the people who'd been waiting outside assailed the small house when they'd heard. That had been enough to get Firuz on their feet and push the others back, closing the bedroom off. But their mind had been whirring, not entirely present as they tried to guide everyone out. They'd never lost a patient before, not like this. Sure, there were the victims of the blood-bruising who'd died, but Firuz heard about those deaths afterward. They weren't in the same room, watching a body behave as it should not. They weren't in the midst of healing, only for it to backfire.

Firuz's throat, as though lined with an abrasive, dried the moisture of their saliva. The blood-bruising. Ahmed. The preserved bodies, which also had damaged blood and overactive marrow at their core. Malika would be pleased to have that mystery solved. "Kofi, there's something—"

"Firuz."

Afsoneh stood by the separating curtain, face pale. She'd brought Kofi back to the uproar, had followed them back to the clinic amid the howling confusion.

They could only imagine what she'd thought, seeing them draped in blood. Firuz had changed their tunic in a daze, taking a sponge from Kofi when it had been offered.

"Should I go home?" She had already poured herself a cup of tea from the samovar on the counter, usually kept running throughout the day for both healers and patients. There were cuts on the back of her hand where she gripped the mug, the angry red of new ones among the healed. How many times had Firuz repeated their warning about not practicing without them? After the incident with Parviz, they'd thought she'd listened. They'd thought it had sunk in: even if it hadn't painted a target on their backs, blood magic could destroy a person from the inside out if they didn't know what they were doing. Afsoneh thought she knew what she was doing, but she didn't, couldn't even call herself a true adept with Firuz's pitiful instruction.

"Firuz?"

"Huh? Oh—yes, that's probably for the best." They didn't like the idea of her walking home by herself, though, even if the sun was still out. "Perhaps Kofi-khan would be kind enough to walk you home when you're ready."

Kofi inclined his head. "I'd be happy to."

Afsoneh nodded, came to sit on Firuz's other side, her shoulder warm against theirs. "Firuz, what . . . happened?"

Firuz pressed chapped lips to her temple, this girl who'd become their sister on top of their ward and trainee. Ahmed had been her friend, after all. "It . . . was some sort of parasite, I think. Or, well, that's what it felt like—a sort of magical parasite, not an organic one. It must have been tethered to his life energy. When I killed it . . ." Words escaped them, unable to reach the heart of the matter. Their sinuses clogged. "Muck bury it. I didn't know—"

"It's not your fault," repeated Kofi. "Drink the tea, they-Firuz. Breathe."

Breathe. Ahmed couldn't breathe anymore. Were all those with the blood-bruising doomed to die because of some incompetent magic? The blood-bruising in the living and the preservation in the dead. Someone was meddling with the lives of others, warping their bodies to remain active past death for a reason unknown.

Someone who, unless something had changed, wasn't at the other clinics.

Firuz's attention fell back on Afsoneh's hands.

But—no. It couldn't be her. Could it? When would Afsoneh have had access to all those people? Her presence at the clinic was usually for the purposes of training or picking something up. Unless she somehow leashed the mechanism to Firuz, it didn't make sense.

The bruises on Parviz's back surfaced in Firuz's mind, unbidden. Was she really risking an entire population to help her best friend? The thought burned behind Firuz's navel. Could she really be capable of harming so many innocent people? It was either that or another, unrelated blood adept in Qilwa.

In a city swarming with Sassanian refugees, how

would Firuz find the culprit? Even if they could, what then? They couldn't very well tell the governor. Back in Dilmun, they would have turned the person over to the elders, washed themself clean of the whole thing. The elders did not vindicate those who misused the centuries-old science; the techniques were guarded closer than a queen's newborn heir, and the wielders underwent a rigorous and feared test to prove their control and prevent exactly this. Firuz still had scars from their own trial. Unless this was a deliberate command to wipe out a portion of the Qilwan population—an indiscriminate disease, to be sure—the blood-bruising had to be unsanctioned use, or else someone the elders had never trained.

And perhaps the bigger question: should Firuz tell Kofi?

Once the plague had settled into the past, most Qilwans viewed anything Sassanian with careful disdain, but not Kofi. He might understand, might help Firuz figure out what to do . . . or else kick them out of his life.

But they didn't need to make the decision now, tired and heartsick as they were. They took Afsoneh's empty cup along with their half-full one to go dump out. "Don't worry about me. If you could take Afsoneh home now, Kofi-khan, I'd appreciate it. I think I'd like to spend some time here, keep my mind occupied."

Kofi considered this, hair swaying in his breeze, before rising. "All right, but take tomorrow off, Firuz-jan. You should rest."

Before he'd finished, they were shaking their head. "No, I'd rather work. Really, Kofi-khan. I'll be fine."

"Hmm. Let's not open until the afternoon, then." He opened the door for Afsoneh when she picked up her bag. "Ready to head home?"

She nodded, worried at her lower lip. "Firuz?"

"Yes?"

She looked over at Kofi, then back at them. "Are you sure you're going to be okay?"

Their lips turned up into what they hoped was a soft smile. They cupped her cheek, stroked the bone defining it. "This is what it means to be a healer. Yes, I'll be okay. Make sure Parviz eats whatever Maadar makes for dinner." If she cooked at all—most days, Firuz came home to a cold stove and two starving teenagers. "Even if it's eggplant."

"Okay. I'll try." Afsoneh gave them a quick hug before following Kofi. "Try to get some sleep, Rooz."

Muck, that nickname hurt. They watched the two of them depart from the window. Kofi bent his head, listening to whatever Afsoneh had to say, nodding and attending to her with what appeared to be his full attention. Firuz knuckled their eyes as they slid the curtain shut. They'd never felt so alone.

Firuz awoke to chanting. As expected, they'd stayed up most of the night, ruminating over Ahmed, then fallen asleep as the sun announced the dawn. They pushed themself from the sofa, rubbing crusty eyes; their mouth tasted rank, the ghost of yesterday's meals. Yawning, they pulled back the curtain to see what the commotion was about.

And bolted up, wishing they were still asleep.

A group—Firuz counted maybe thirty people—thronged outside the clinic, fists in the air. In front of them stood three city guards, batons aloft; a fourth, with the captain's lion insignia stamped on their armor, held out their hands, shouting at the crowd. Kofi stood next to them, arms similarly spread in a placating gesture.

Firuz opened the clinic door, squinting as they stepped outside in the mid-morning sun. "Kofi, what—"

"Murderer!" screamed the person at the front of the crowd. One of the guards pushed them back, and Firuz realized with a sickening jerk it was Ahmed's mother. Had a single day aged her so much, or had Firuz not noticed before the gray hairs, the wrinkles, the hunched posture? Ahmed's sweet, calmer mother —what a moniker, at a time like this—wasn't with her wife. The pain of this woman, the one Firuz had dubbed "no nonsense," cracked open for all to witness. "You killed my son!"

"What?" Firuz tried to push between the guards, but they wouldn't let them through. "No, I didn't! Ahmed died—"

She clapped her hands over her ears, shaking. "I saw what you did in there! Our people still know the Sassanian curse!" She jabbed a finger towards Firuz. "You've come from your skies-forsaken land to take ours away from us again. The plague wasn't enough for you, so you had to go for my Ahmed! May the Nameless hide Ous name from your corrupted mind!"

The others cried out in support. Kofi sighed and spun a finger. A gust of wind tore through the crowd, pushing them back from the clinic door. "Everyone, please, return to your homes." The breeze he controlled amplified his volume. "Umm Ahmed, please come inside and talk with us. It is clear you are grieving—"

"Do not mock me!" Her face twisted in fury as spittle flew from her mouth. "I know what I saw, Kofi-healer, and if you think you can protect that murdering, bird-loving scum—"

Firuz tried to reach for the older woman, but she cringed away as though they'd threatened her. They stepped back, holding up their hands. "I didn't kill him, khanoom, I swear. I was trying to save—"

The flocked neighbors parted. Ahmed's other mother shuffled through, her steps swaying, her hair disheveled. "Nia, enough. They did the best they could."

Nia snarled, whirling on her wife. "You saw what they did! The way they cut into him—the blood! Everywhere!"

"I saw a healer doing a job I do not understand, using a tool I understand even less."

"Magic does not look like that!" hissed Nia. "I do

not have to be a user to know this, Amara!"

Nia-mama will have words, that's for sure, Ahmed had said months ago with a laugh, before the blood-bruising had wrecked him, before Firuz had felt his beating heart stutter still in a room showered with blood. Back when his only concern had been fractures from a failed attempt to win Afsoneh's affections, not a disease so ravaging his body was unrecognizable in its final breaths.

Exhaustion almost sank Firuz to their knees. The back of their head ached.

"Please, come home." Amara gestured to the murmuring and shifting crowd. "This is not the way. What happened in that room led to the same result and might have regardless of what magic was used. Please, Nia." A tear slipped down her cheek. "Not now."

Amara's weary manner moved Nia to cover her mouth. When she turned to meet Firuz's helpless stare, she dropped her hands and glared. The look ran deep with hatred, and Firuz cowered. "You will pay for this. Mark my words, your crimes will haunt your steps. Nameless Creator make it so." Then she wrapped an arm around her wife's shoulder and turned, leaving through the parted crowd. After a shift, some murmurs, the others also trickled away, some turning to shoot Firuz more dirty looks.

Firuz sagged against the clinic entrance. This was going to have repercussions. "Skies."

The captain of the guard turned to Firuz, their mustache twitching. "The governor's going to hear about this. You'd best be here when we come to question you."

For the first time, Firuz's thumb was already bleeding and halfway towards the guard before they realized what they were doing. They withdrew, heart hammering so hard they were sure their ribs would burst. "I didn't kill him."

The guard didn't appear fazed. "We'll launch an investigation. Whatever you did nearly caused a riot. Now"—the captain stepped closer, staring down at Firuz from on high—"are you going to set this story straight or not?"

"Captain," said Kofi, "if you would, please interrogate my assistant at a later time. As a personal favor."

The captain glowered, shaking their head. "This is bad business, Kofi. I'd watch out if I were you." They shot Firuz another suspicious look, muttering something sounding an awful lot like an ethnic slur, and gestured to the other guards to put away their weapons. "Let's go."

Firuz watched the small group retreat, barely feeling the tug at their sleeve. Then the tugs became a yank, and Firuz huffed at Kofi. "What?"

"Inside," he murmured. "To be safe."

In they went, and Kofi locked the door and wrenched the curtain tight. "I don't trust this is over," he said. "Not with your blood-bruising happening too. Come with me; I want to show you something."

"Uhm, okay." Firuz followed Kofi into the supply room. Kofi snapped his fingers to light the lantern hanging from the ceiling. "Can I ask you something?"

Kofi knelt on the ground and ran his hands along the wood. Firuz hadn't bothered to explore the underground space since Kofi had appeared from it during Afsoneh's training, but perhaps Kofi had done some of the work he'd said was needed to make the space useable. Kofi's fingers found the gap, and he lifted the cover. "Yes, what is it?"

The smell of wet earth rose to meet Firuz's nostrils. "What did she mean when she said the Sassanian curse?"

"Oh." Kofi rose to get a candle and its holder from the back shelf. "It's said when your people took ours over, they made a pact with a dark god to gain powers over life. They used those powers to bind us to the empire so we were no longer our own peoples. Here, hold this."

Firuz took the candlestick as Kofi lifted the wooden ladder propped against the wall and lowered it into the waiting darkness. Firuz had assumed the ladder was for maintenance work. "But Sassanid stopped existing three hundred years ago. Why hold on to that still? It's not like we came in with scimitar and spells—ours was a cultural empire. Besides, Qilwa was the one who betrayed us to help Dilmun."

"Betrayed?" Kofi set the ladder in place, jiggling it to make sure of its security, before rocking back on his heels. "Firuz-jan, Sassanid took us against our will. Declared us to be Sassanian too, demanding their culture as superior to ours. We were not vassals eager to be so; we were a flourishing monarchy. That is a betrayal too, is it not? To take your neighbor's lands as your own?"

Firuz thought back through history, as if a specific memory could make sense of Kofi's perspective. The elders made it clear not everything about Old Sassanid had been great, but the advancements, the knowledge, the flourishing of societies—did that not count? "But Dilmun was the one who didn't keep their promise. At least Sassanid let the Qilwan government stay in power."

"The tribute exacted by the empire allowed our continued subjugation under Dilmun later." The oil lamp from the ceiling danced shadows on Kofi's face. "So goes the argument, anyway."

"Qilwans are some of the richest people in the world!"

"Think, Firuz. Do Sassanians not resent Dilmunis in much the same way?" Firuz had to admit Kofi had them there. Kofi tapped his chest. "It's a matter of the heart and mind both. All peoples are proud, and all want to be their own. First we were part of Sassanid, and then Dilmun, the only part of the empire they did not free. It is only now, one thousand years later, that we can be ourselves without another's oversight."

What could Firuz say to that? No wonder Qilwans were so terrified of the flood of refugees from the mainland. As though their hard-won independence would be tossed aside; as though the sacrifices of Qilwan freedom fighters to secure it were pointless. No, it was more complicated than Sassanians being victims here. What did it mean to belong to a people who had once subjugated another before becoming subjugated themselves?

Before Firuz could come up with a response, Kofi gave them a wry smile. "My love and I used to have this debate, too, for many years." He held out his hand. "The candle."

"What? Oh." Firuz passed it over. "Where does this lead?"

"I'll show you. Follow me."

Kofi descended into the gaping hole. After he was gone from view, a snap echoed up, and a light flickered from the candle. So there was enough space down there for more than one person, enough space for Kofi to have something to show them. Despite misgivings—the back of Firuz's mind warned of being buried alive—Firuz headed down themselves.

The air was musty and choked with dirt. No circulation here at all, and Firuz shivered, arms breaking out into a shock of gooseflesh, and tried not to hyperventilate; they'd never realized they had such an intense fear of being trapped. Perhaps this claustrophobia was why they'd never made time to check down here.

Kofi surveyed the area, hands on his hips. "I still haven't figured a good way to make this space useable for the long term, but it works for now. This way."

As Kofi led them down the hall, Firuz dug their sleeve-sewn needle into their palm, a comforting instinct. The dirt tunnel stretched out before them, a strong mildew scent permeating the limited space. Firuz breathed through their mouth and tried not to think about all that could collapse onto them, the dirt and wooden boards and clinic shelves and books and—

"Here we are." The air behind them cooled as Kofi flung out an arm, lamps startling to life to reveal a laboratory the likes of which Firuz had not seen anywhere else in Qilwa.

Beakers and buckets and tubs; shelves with carefully labeled ingredients like crystallized ginger, dried tulsi, fennel fruits, even zireh-ye kuhi, the black cumin pods grown in Dilmun; tables stacked with books; a multilens set at the ready. Firuz itched to try it, as they'd only seen a set with multiple lenses once before, or to distill a solution in the glassware set up for such purposes, or to light the burners awaiting a flame—to tinker with any of the equipment here, their favorite kind of toys.

"Kofi," they marveled, their fear of entrapment for now tempered with the large room, "this is . . ."

Then they spotted the chair.

Even at first glance, it was not ordinary. From the arms dangled leather straps, and under, cotton lined carved moatlike gutters. The legs stretched into flat footrests with more straps. No cushion lined the back or bottom. Indeed, the back was basically a frame with crossed beams for support, and sitting on the chair itself was a spiked metal cage the size of a coconut. The only thing unusual about the setup was that it was clean instead of covered in the brown rust of old blood.

Firuz had not seen a dastgah in over ten years.

"Where did you get that?" Their voice choked. Memories they'd thought long buried resurfaced—images of their mentor binding their arms, placing their hand in the cage; the taste of wood as Firuz bit into a plank to hold back screams; reuniting broken knuckles and shredded tissue minute after agonizing minute; a denied request to switch to their foot when they'd said they wanted to become a healer and needed a steady hand.

A silent promise they'd made to Afsoneh to never put her through Sassanian blood magic training, which always led back to this.

"One of my trips to Dilmun." Kofi's answer brought Firuz back to the present. "You recognize it." It was not a question.

Perhaps they'd blanched. Or maybe they'd clenched their fist—no, they were holding their hand to their chest, the hand that had been broken in too many places too many times. "Do you know what it is?"

"Yes."

Then there was no point in lying anymore. Holding back a gag as their memory-blood dripped into gutters under another chair's arms—the chair was clean, the chair was clean, *the chair was clean*—Firuz finally peeled away to turn to Kofi. He was leaning against a workbench, watching them. Firuz wavered, even as the images from their past dwindled; they steadied themself with a sharp prod of the small incision in their palm. "Why do you know what it is?"

"I could ask you the same."

"I think you know why. How long have you known?"

"Guessed," corrected Kofi. "Your eyes were the first giveaway, but you were so adamant about structuralism, I thought it perhaps a thing of your past. Then I learned in Dilmun it's risky and tricky to do magical alignments unless you're a blood mage."

"Adept," corrected Firuz automatically. That conversation with Parviz—so Kofi had known then, after all. "Mage means you have certain skills."

Kofi dismissed this with a wave. "That is beside my point, Firuz-jan, which I think you know." They did. "Even without your mentioning the magic, it seemed fair to guess you were passingly familiar with your people's science, if not more. But then, with what happened yesterday . . ."

Firuz flinched, clasped their hand tighter. "I was trying to save him."

"I believe you. And I understand why you did not tell me." Kofi sat on top of the workbench, hands bracing his weight as he leaned forward. "But I knew it was time to show you, and for us to have this chat. So the question is, where do we go from here?"

Firuz looked back at the chair. For a beat, they saw again the rivulets of blood flowing down the arms, feet bound to the legs. "When did you say you brought this back?"

"I didn't, but it was early last year. Why?"

The lab was familiar. Firuz took a moment to place it: it resembled a smaller version of the one in the royal palace of Dilmun, which they'd glimpsed once as a child on a trip with the elders. The beakers and lenses weren't for show; they were used to separate out the components of blood, creating new spells in doing so. The more one fathomed a thing, the more one could control it. *Magic is mostly a working of the will.* And indeed, a beaker atop a closed burner held an opaque, pus-yellow liquid, so Firuz couldn't help but wonder . . .

"If you don't know what you're doing, blood magic can kill you." Maybe they should have taken Kofi's offer to not come into work today. Maybe they could have avoided being here, having to confront this possibility. "Or worse." They moved towards the filled beaker, fingers trailing on the table. "It's remarkable you're alive."

"I am, yes." Kofi sighed. "Others were not so lucky. Those were accidents. I had no idea it would spread."

Others. The bodies. The blood-bruising. Something different about their clinic. How had Firuz not guessed it before? Kofi was the most dedicated healer they'd ever met. He'd stop at nothing to find every way, unconventional or dangerous or not, to help his patients.

"So when I came to you about the blood-bruising . . . ?" With the back of their palm, Firuz touched the glass on the bench. Cold, and what was inside puffed out sweet smells, like an illness. "What are you trying to accomplish? Why tell me now?"

"I didn't know the blood-bruising was my doing, actually, not at first." Kofi hopped to the floor, meandered towards the chair. It took immense self-control for Firuz not to leap out to stop him. "I was looking for a cure for the plague, one we could disseminate widely. So much needless death. So much waste." He reached the chair, plucked up the dastgah with the tips of his fingers. Firuz could not be far enough from that mucking instrument. "And then the governor began to buy out the clinics. And then she interfered, time and time again, with how we treat our patients. And then a grieving mother came thundering at our door, and the guards threatened to take you away because you did your best to save a dying boy. I want to show you what I've been working on." Kofi replaced the dastgah on its earlier spot. "Bring the beaker too."

Everything about this vibrated a wrongness Firuz couldn't deny. Yet Kofi's face wasn't sinister or overcast; it was bright, hopeful. The face of their mentor, who had saved hundreds if not thousands of Sassanians over the past year. The mentor they'd finally, achingly, learned to trust.

Firuz's body moved, and when they focused back, they were next to Kofi, next to the skies-forsaken chair, holding up the glassware.

Kofi withdrew a vial from his pocket. "Hold this. What do you sense?"

The liquid inside was a deep, dark maroon, but Firuz knew what it was. Despite their misgivings, they took the vial. The blood shifted, sang—and faltered. "Whomever you took this from was sick at the time. This is tainted."

Kofi inclined his head. "A loaded word, they-Firuz." The nickname brought them no comfort. "Now watch."

He took the beaker from Firuz, placed it on the table, and slid the vial into a nearby stand. He grabbed droppers and an empty vial from the shelf before returning. With a flourish, Kofi extracted the isolated infection, the pus thick as it teased its way up the dropper, emptied it into the clean vial, then added the sick blood. Swirling the contents, he extended it to Firuz. "Now what do you feel?"

Fingers closed around the glass. The blood shifted— and that was it. Firuz gaped at the vial, then at Kofi. "Did it . . . kill the infection?"

Kofi grinned.

Firuz worked through the mechanism's possibilities, but the most plausible leapt at them. Make a body think it was under attack, and it would mobilize its immunities into the blood. Take that blood and apply it to another disease as a treatment. And the corresponding mistakes, all the steps it would take to get to this moment—place an imperfect product into another, and that body would mobilize against the intruder, churning out new, maybe faulty blood and overworking itself until its demise; or, alternatively, the body would attack itself as the effects of the spell lingered. Either way, it could lead to the same symptoms: first, extreme fatigue, as imperfect blood could not carry nutrients and the air one breathed, and regular bruising, as such blood could not clot; then, preservation after death, as the spell found more to fix. As for the spread, well—a spell needed an energy source, and an unstable spell might be easy to mutate, easy to reach to another and hook into them as the new host.

But this, as the finished product—blood that attacked illness and wiped it out without a trace?

Firuz lifted the vial to the light, as if doing so would illuminate more.

How remarkable, using the body's own defenses against a disease by magical means instead of natural. Limitless potential for so much healing—what would it mean to use a dying individual to build hope for the living? The sick healing the sick, instead of sewing the burial shroud, creating a lifeline where before there was only cut rope. Weakened bodies could be strengthened; failing hearts and lungs and kidneys bolstered; and in a place overrun by the unwanted ill, healers could work without losing resources they deemed too precious for those who could not pay.

Blood magic could branch from its history at last.

A lifetime of training punched Firuz in the throat, ensnaring their wonder and choking it. Their fascination with the implications aside, there was a reason the science was so heavily guarded. Its rediscovery had caused the end of a conquest in exchange for the beginnings of a war—a war Dilmun was still waging. Sure, things had been peaceful for a time, but then a monster appeared in the sky. Then a genocide began. Blood magic was as much a death sentence as it was a potential gift, dooming more than the user, should a mishap arise. Hadn't its misuse here proven as much?

No matter how many Sassanians Kofi had saved, so many more were dying. And not only Sassanians— anyone residing on the island. The blood-bruising wreaked havoc in whomever it settled irrespective of ethnicity, sank its fangs in to release a fatal venom. And the number of cases kept increasing. Such an imperfect science was blood magic, no matter how the elders pretended otherwise, and relinquishing these tools to untrained healers in the hopes of helping was a recipe for disaster.

The vial taunted Firuz, dared them to discount the risks in favor of the possibilities.

Skies, Kofi was trying to help. He *had* helped—the clinic's hundreds of patients were too clear a sign. Who else would fight the most powerful person in the city in order to serve those whose bodies would otherwise clog the sewers, poison the water, remind Qilwa its freedom was not so secure? Kofi was Qilwan through and through, yet when it came to his patients, he would help not for money or fame but because it was the right thing to do. Because healing was his creed and calling.

But was this the way?

"The two of us could revolutionize our profession." Kofi shone with confidence, brimming with excitement. "We could make a difference in this city. Prove your people and mine can live and work together to benefit all. Show the governor how wrong she is." Kofi took Firuz's hand, turned it over. A featherlight touch ghosted against the puncture from their needle. "No more of this. No more secrets."

The touch was more comforting than it had any right to be, even as every bit of Firuz warned them to flee. "This . . . isn't right, Kofi."

"I know it might be difficult to think about—"

"It's more than that. This goes against everything I was ever taught. Everything . . . skies, Kofi, you're a healer!" Firuz stepped away from Kofi's grasp and ran a hand through their hair, beginning to pace. "You know death changes the body. That changes the magic." It was why even the most powerful of blood mages couldn't raise armies of the dead, why blood adepts trained on themselves and not on corpses.

"And why can't we use that change to our advantage?" Kofi opened his arms to gesture to the lab around them. "I've been working down here for months. Imagine how much more we can get done with the two of us. We can create a new blood magic, one without the history and baggage of empire, one my people do not fear and yours no longer have to hide."

So much hope. So much potential. So much room for error, with an entire city at stake.

"Think on it." Kofi clasped his hands together. "This is a chance at a new magic, a chance to unite our peoples and our cultures, should we care to. Forget the past of your people and mine; forget the histories of Qilwan and Sassanian and Dilmuni. What have our people done for us, Firuz?"

"The elders—"

"Your elders," spat Kofi, "oh yes, your elders, your skies-cursed elders." His vitriol took Firuz aback; the only time Kofi sounded this bitter was when discussing the governor. "Tell me, how have they helped you over the past two years? What has listening to them taught you other than pain and fear?" Kofi's chin jutted towards Firuz's hand. "You rub that when you think. The bones still ache, do they not? I know all about your elders and their methods. I saw what the memories of them did to my love. I see what they do to you."

Kofi's love? Kofi's late partner, whom Firuz knew was Sassanian and not much else. So hu'd been a blood magic user too, or more likely, an adept. Firuz tugged on their collar. "You don't know—"

"Don't I?" Kofi tossed his head. "Your elders chose to hide these secrets, pretend it makes your people special and different. Perhaps they plot a new empire of their own; has that ever occurred to you?" Kofi's voice picked up speed as he talked, growing louder. "Maybe whatever is killing your people is their doing, a fake danger to consolidate their power. Or maybe the Dilmuni queen minds a threat when she sees one. Your elders are the ones to blame for this—our city's problems. Think, Firuz. What a difference the two of us could make despite those people who still hold you back." Kofi motioned to the dastgah, again with his chin. "The people who put you through that."

Firuz stared at the metal that glinted instead of rusted. The elders had all gone through the same training once, knew the pain and damage it caused. As an adolescent, Firuz had questioned this, and their mentor had smoothed their then-long hair, braided it down their back as zhe answered. *"Firuz-jan, you cannot appreciate the dangers a tool possesses unless you are hurt by it. Only then can you learn how to use it properly to prevent such pain. How else can we promise the world we pose no threat?"*

No threat. What a comfortable lie. Was Firuz truly better than other blood magic users if they thought themself capable of what Kofi wanted, no matter how tempting it was? No matter how much sense the logic made?

People had died to get Kofi to this point.

Firuz stepped back. "I can't, Kofi. I'm sorry."

His disappointment hurt more than any injury could. "But you've seen what's happened here," Kofi said. "You know—"

"I do know. I know exactly. Which is why I can't condone this." Nor could Firuz allow it to continue, but how to get Kofi to stop?

"Firuz," pleaded Kofi again. "Please, please think on it. Don't make a rash decision we will both regret."

Oh, to abandon this room, this plan, to renounce everything in the hopes of safety. What did Kofi see on their face, in the gauntness of their cheeks, in the slouch of their posture? "Don't get me wrong, Kofi. I hear what you're saying, and I even agree with some of it." More than they'd like to admit. "But you don't know what it was like to go through that training." Another Firuz could have met Kofi's hope with defiance, could have scoffed and denounced this plan, but this Firuz cradled their broken heart, offered it to the man who had been mentor and friend and family. "You have no idea what it's like to be a blood magic user by affinity. No clue what our culture does and doesn't condone. All this?" Firuz gestured around them. "All this is exactly why the elders don't let just anyone study blood magic. All of this is exactly what they've spent centuries trying to prevent. I will not go against my people and put this entire city at even more risk, no matter how they've hurt me. I can't."

So much of Firuz saw the logic in Kofi's plan, but the dangers outweighed the potential good. Were they being rash in denying Kofi this experiment? They didn't think so. Not when Malika burned dozens of bodies each week. Not when a teen's blood was yet to dry from their hands.

Kofi spent a long moment looking at Firuz, a moment Firuz thought would stretch past the two of them and spin out into the universe. Around them, the room buzzed with anticipation, as though the contents of the jars would spring to life, as though the extracted and multiplied pus could goop up into a monster of its own making. What a brilliant laboratory this was, from the mind of a brilliant man, an environmentalist whose talent for healing had saved so many lives.

Then Kofi caved in on himself. "I see. Well, then. Forgive me for this, Firuz."

A tingling heat shot up from Firuz's palm; they yelped, clutched their wrist. The small slit from the needle reddened, and the wooziness hit them before they understood. Kofi hadn't taken their hand earlier to make a point; he'd done it to gain access to their blood. They swayed, should have been able to fight back, but sleep was too natural to overcome. Firuz's knees buckled before they blacked out.

Voices woke them, the damp air swollen with the taste of buried dirt. Firuz groaned, coughed, turned their cheek.

"They're awake!" hissed a familiar voice. "Grab the towel."

"Parviz?" Firuz blinked, squinting. Parviz dabbed their forehead with a wet cloth, but Firuz could not make out his expression, so unfocused were the edges of their vision. They could barely feel the cloth against their skin. "What are you doing here?" Nausea crested through them; they bent over and vomited onto their lap, where a towel was conveniently placed. It was mostly spittle and stomach acid, but they whimpered.

"What did he do to them?" Parviz sounded frantic, and Firuz felt hands lifting their chin.

"I don't know, maybe some kind of poison?" That was Afsoneh; Firuz tried to locate her. Why was their vision so hazy? Mud, they really needed lenses sooner rather than later. Their head spun, and they moaned, leaned back. They were sitting in a chair, wooden arms with familiar gutters . . .

Firuz shot up, stumbled, vomited again on the floor. Parviz caught them before they could fall. "Hey, easy."

"Do you know what happened?" Afsoneh came forward to support Firuz on the other side. "You didn't come home last night. Kofi said you hadn't been in when he arrived, but I . . . I could feel you, down here."

"Last night?" The ache in Firuz's head became a pounding, a hammer to the back of their neck. "I—muck, where is he?"

But Afsoneh and Parviz weren't looking at their face. "Firuz," whispered their brother. "Look."

Firuz followed his gaze. One of their arms was purple from the elbow up, and the rest of their bronzed olive skin was peppered in familiar brown marks. Parviz pointed to a set resembling fingers. "That just happened."

"Muck take it and bury it in mud," whispered Firuz. "The two of you need to get out of here and away from me."

Afsoneh shook her head. "We can't leave you here." Her attention was trained behind them. "You'll be tied up again." Firuz glanced back over their shoulder and shuddered at the chair. Rope was discarded around it, hacked through with an object too blunt to cut cleanly.

"If you lean on me, we should be able to get you back up." Parviz frowned up at Firuz. "Though you'll get more bruises."

"Bruises I can handle." Blood-bruising less so. This laboratory was the best chance they had at curing themself; they could already feel their strength leeching away. Had Kofi infected them in their sleep? Why was it moving so much faster inside them? They could feel the pounding of their heart slamming against their ribs, the increased turbulence in their veins and arteries, the way their lungs trapped and refused to relinquish air.

But they had an idea, one Kofi had given them. Firuz didn't believe in the Shahbaaz's blessing, didn't believe in a god that hadn't kept their people safe. But Firuz did believe in the science that was magic, and that would have to be enough.

They limped over to the bench. They tried not to think about how much smaller the room felt with three people and the crowded instruments, tried to ignore the fear of the room's potential collapse. There was no time.

"Rooz, we have to go," urged Parviz.

"Listen to me. Whatever he did, I'm dying." Afsoneh gasped; Parviz paled, stepped a foot back. "This is my best shot at making it. You two, get out of here. Get . . ." Muck. The city guard was out of the question; even if someone did believe two Sassanian kids, Firuz was already a suspect. But there was someone who would help, maybe even believe them about Kofi. "My friend she-Malika, the mortician. You remember her, right? She lives behind the mortuary."

"I'll go." Parviz's voice was firm, unwavering.

"Afsoneh, stay and help Firuz. I'll go get her." She nodded.

"Dudush . . ." There was so much Firuz wanted to say to their brother. So many apologies.

But Parviz glared at them. "Don't 'dudush' me. I'm still mad at you." He hesitated, then sprung forward to kiss Firuz's cheek. "Don't die on me," he whispered. "I need you, Rooz. Don't die."

And then he ran.

Firuz choked back tears. They couldn't afford to waste any energy. "Magelet," they rasped. "Time for an impromptu lesson."

Parviz had not yet returned by the time Firuz separated their blood into its parts. Despite the increased pressure in their veins and difficulties clotting, the extraction was sluggish, oozing down their forearm as they squeezed their skin, held it over a beaker to collect. As they divided the blood into vials, Afsoneh found a density separator gathering dust in a cabinet; she balanced the tubes before activating the etched runes and cranking the rusty handle until a dark pellet coalesced on the bottom of each and a yellowish-clear layer formed on top. It took several tries to split them into the third layer, a middle white one for extraction.

Firuz had read this was some component of blood that fought infection. The blood-bruising was not a true infection, but it might be able to be treated like one, smothered like ash did worm-infested roots. The same way Firuz had smothered what had lain inside Ahmed, only to fail to save his life.

Parviz did not return when Firuz had Afsoneh multiply out these elements. Blood easily mobilized to her will, and with enough concentrated samples along with vials of her own to use as prerequisite material, she encouraged its growth, even though Firuz worried it might not work without marrow, might somehow permanently drain her own life's energy to do so. She worked with alacritous speed, allowing the curls of her hair to crumple to dust in a reaction Firuz had never seen before. Her explanation had been, simply, that she stored energy there, and did not mind its uneven, half-shorn appearance. Given the lifelessness of hair, Firuz didn't know what she meant.

And Parviz still did not return when Firuz tested the concoction on more of their blood and found it to be blood-bruising free. Unexpected pride in Afsoneh's abilities crested through them as they examined the healthy blood.

"Perhaps you've come around to my line of thinking."

Firuz whirled; Afsoneh obeyed their instinctive tug behind them, although the gesture seemed useless. "Kofi."

Kofi walked through the entrance of the lab, almost sauntering. When had he arrived, and how long had he watched Firuz struggle? Surely Afsoneh would have noticed if he'd been there long, though that she hadn't noticed at all was a testament to how focused she'd been. He seemed paler than usual but was otherwise the same Kofi Firuz had known for almost two years, the same Kofi they'd almost trusted with their biggest secret.

"Your trainee found you. It seems I underestimated her as well." Had Kofi aged so much in a day? Had he always had wisps of white in the cloud atop his head? Had the lines around his eyes and mouth always been so dark? When Firuz had noticed this of Ahmed's mother, it made sense with her grief; but why Kofi? "I was hoping the illness might change your mind."

The wound of the betrayal rankled, festering and stinking. "You tried to kill me."

"It was not my intention for you to die, merely to get sick." When had Kofi become this ruthless, this reckless? Firuz refused to believe they hadn't known who their mentor was deep down. This had to be a manifestation of desperately unsound judgment. The city had driven Kofi to this point, and perhaps Firuz's refusal had made him snap. "Now we have a bigger matter to contend with, which is what to do with you." He shook his head. "I'm sorry it's come to this, Firuz. Please believe me when I say you have been as close to me as family, and I love you dearly. But I believe this work will change the city for the better, and my patients need me more than you do."

A heartbeat before it happened, Firuz realized Kofi meant to fight them.

The dirt floor of the lab swirled around their feet as Kofi splayed his palms out, tracing circles in the air. Firuz shoved Afsoneh away, then used what little arm strength they had to slide across the table and onto the other side. The wind shifted; Kofi used it like a tornado, lifting dirt higher into a swirling stream before it branched into two thickened limbs, packed with dirt. One branch pinned Afsoneh against a workbench as the other pressed Firuz to the ground. Their skin bruised under the impact; the pain of aching, straining muscles pulsed through them. But what suffocated them was the utter helplessness of being bound and trapped, surely a precursor to the building's collapse.

"I'm going to get the guard." The dirt hardened around Firuz's limbs, drying into mud as Kofi lifted the moisture underground to pack the top. "I imagine after Ahmed, they'll understand what they see here. I'm sorry."

A glass cylinder flew through the air and smashed above Kofi's head. Afsoneh was grabbing whatever she could reach from the bench and hurling it at him while she broke through her restraints. Firuz suppressed their catastrophizing—she was their best bet for survival—and yelled that the scalpel was on the tabletop. No time for surprise; she snatched it up and slashed her palms as Kofi dove down, snapping his fingers. The dirt around Afsoneh and Firuz sprouted roots, tunneling towards their wrists and ankles. Firuz had not the strength to be shocked at magic a different Kofi would have condemned. Afsoneh squirmed of reach, losing her shoes in the process, before rushing over to Firuz. She secured her arms under theirs and pulled them out of the winding plant's hold as they kicked themself free.

Kofi did not give them a moment's reprieve; arms outstretched like wings, he clenched his fists, and much of the glassware around the room, the beakers and tubes and jars and stirrers, shattered, and the contents rose as though alive, and the splinters and shards readied. The glittering fragments dove towards Firuz, who dug for energy reserves they weren't sure they still had, but Afsoneh flung out her own arms. Droplets of her blood sprayed out in a protective arc frozen in midair, a barrier repelling the roots and glass and whatever else Kofi had to throw at them.

Firuz had definitely not taught her that.

"I can't hold it for long," she managed, as Kofi observed them, dismissing his makeshift weapons to cascade to the dirt with light *thumps*. "Do something!"

Muck, Firuz was running out of time; the blood-bruising weakened them with every passing moment. Their entire body was rebelling: their head hammered against their skull, their calves seized, and their breaths panted in laborious gasps. Firuz grabbed their amulet from around their neck and slashed the sharp end down their palm. They'd never used their pendant for this purpose, but it was the real reason they'd forged it, in case of an emergency. And this was an emergency.

When the barrier fizzled and popped, blood raining on silent ground, Kofi jumped into action, summoning swirling winds with twirling index fingers. Afsoneh pushed herself up and sprinted, catching him by surprise when she slammed into him. He staggered and tripped, falling onto his back. Firuz dove for their mentor but didn't bother with anything fancy in their weakened state. Instead, they swiped their palm, cut further on the thorny roots, against Kofi's lips and rolled away, shoving their magic into him. Kofi's arms snapped to his side, removing his ability to channel environmental forces efficiently. He struggled against the invisible constraints.

Afsoneh's bloody hand snagged Firuz's own, and her magic swelled within them as she burrowed into their link to Kofi. She seized his blood—and in the process, Firuz's.

The mucking dangers of untrained blood magic.

Firuz's throat constricted; they wheezed, grasping at the invisible cord. Their hold on Kofi loosened. He, too, was gagging, pushing himself up as he tried to breathe and crawl to the other two. Apparently in the process Afsoneh had also bound herself, because she sank to the floor and choked alongside the adults. Firuz flailed their arms to break her concentration; her spell snapped hard enough to ricochet energy through the links. Firuz's teeth chattered as they wheezed, sucking in great gulps of air.

The whole ordeal took only long enough for Kofi to reach the two of them on his hands and knees. Before Firuz could stop him, Kofi surged towards Afsoneh, the bigger threat, and grabbed her bleeding wrist.

Firuz broke into a cold sweat as their heart began to race. Something wriggled in their consciousness, a burning in their magic. Afsoneh's magic joined to theirs usually felt like a stream of cool water, but this felt like a colony of fire ants.

They only realized they were crying out when their scratchy vocal cords faltered. Kofi wasn't only mucking about in their magic; he was in their body too. Kofi was combining his skills as a healer with un-trained blood magic in order to—

No, wait. The rational, detached part of Firuz's mind, the one developed under years of training, traced the origins of the pulses shooting through them. These effects were incidental; Kofi was targeting Afsoneh. And he was . . . muck, he was boiling her blood, or at least attempting to as she fought back, and her linked magic to Firuz passed the resonant energies on to them.

They weren't the only one screaming.

Firuz writhed on the ground, clawing at every un-covered inch of their skin as though doing so would put out the heat in their veins. A dull haze washed over their vision, pressing on them to surrender to the pain and pass out. Unable to see Afsoneh, even as they screeched for her; unable to see Kofi, even as his name echoed in their head, Firuz grabbed the energy in their blood to snap the link tethering the three of them. It felt as meaningful as abandoning one's home to avoid a genocide, only to die in the gutters.

Links could be forged in a single direction, but Firuz had never mastered doing so. *Think of it as a porous membrane*, their old mentor had tried to teach them, *one where some things can pass*—Firuz's power, in this case—*while another cannot*—Kofi's. If they could erect an energetic barrier between Kofi and Afsoneh, such that Firuz could work through her but Kofi could not retaliate . . .

From beside them, Afsoneh struggled against Kofi's grip, her own shrieks climbing as blisters erupted around the wrist of one hand, up her forearm, and then the intense pain inside Firuz vanished. Their vision cleared. The sudden absence was almost as unbearable as the onslaught, but it was enough to remember the old adage, *magic is mostly a working of the will*, and the truth of the saying finally clicked in Firuz's detached mind—the universe would shape energy along its necessary paths as long as one stood steady. How exhilarating to take the strength found in Afsoneh's magic—was this how she felt every time she called upon it?—to wall themself off in one direction, set the same barrier between her and Kofi, and then skim through their own blood to gather the essence of the accelerated blood-bruising. Borrowed power to harness unnatural energy.

Compacting the potency and strength of the disease, Firuz shoved it through Afsoneh and into Kofi, and Kofi alone.

Despite being on his knees already, Kofi collapsed on the ground so violently the dirt underneath him gave way. Afsoneh kicked herself away from him, shaking and sobbing as she pulled herself behind

Firuz and clutched their shirt. Kofi tried to push himself up but fell as though shoved from above. Up and down twice more, and Firuz shivered, quivering jaw aching, taking comfort in the warmth huddled behind them. It was like Kofi was on a string, a puppet in a sick dance, but Firuz couldn't register what they were seeing, what exactly was—

Skies above.

Kofi's blood was eating through his skin, the *click-clack* of bones rattling as his spine arched up and then in, up and then in. First spittle and then blood foamed at his mouth; his eyes rolled to the back of his head, revealing whites; snot poured from his nose as his body spasmed. Kofi screamed as steam rose from him, flaying open every breach. Everyday cuts peeled back to show pink muscle, vessels bursting. One collarbone snapped through his skin, and then the other, as sinew swelled and boiled away as if dropped in acid. Audible pops burst through the air as cartilage released gases bubbling inside.

This was not what Firuz had meant to do—what *had* they meant to do? Stop Kofi at all costs? They dragged themself over, but it was far too late. Kofi's neck snapped as his head rotated around to watch his assistant. His tongue lolled as his eyeballs stared up, jaw crumbling as Firuz cupped the broken face. The useless tongue flapped, the top teeth moving as though in speech, before it and the rest of him dissolved completely. Even his bones crumbled to ash when Firuz moved to pick one up, as if he'd never been there at all.

"Oh, Kofi," they whispered, tears already blurring their sight and dripping down their chin. "This should never have happened." They tried to scoop up what remained of him, but it trickled through their fingers.

"Firuz." Afsoneh wiped her mouth with the back of her charred-looking hand. Vomit pooled at her knees. "We have to get out of here. We have—we have to—"

They leaned against a table leg and reached, holding her as she wept into their shirt, mindful of her injuries. "We should both drink the cure." They tried to blink back blurry vision, their head exploding with every movement. "We should—"

"What in the name of independence happened here?" demanded a voice Firuz was so sure wouldn't make it. "Nameless Creator protect me. Firuz?"

"Malika." They strained to find her in the blur in front of them. They could make her out as she came closer, Parviz dogging her heels. He looked around at the destroyed lab before finding Firuz, and they were sure the relief in his face was real. Firuz tried to smile. "I found out where the blood-bruising and your bodies were coming from."

What was perhaps more shocking than Malika believing Firuz was her willingness to help. She and

Firuz debated whether there was any point in going to the guard or the governor and ultimately decided it was less than a good idea.

"Still, this feels a bit extreme," she remarked, spreading the flammables. "Can't believe I'm a party to this."

"I hear that's what friends are for." Firuz massaged their throat. The taste of the bitter brine of their cure still lingered. They were so weary, the last of their energy spent in healing Afsoneh's injuries with her own help.

"Yeah, well, Kofi told me ages ago he was experimenting with a plague cure. But this—this is something else entirely. I have more bodies not rotting in my morgue than I have room for. If doing this makes sure this cursed research never gets out, then I'm all for it." Then she regarded the two teens, drummed her fingers against her hip. "Still irresponsible to bring your child siblings into it, if you ask me."

Parviz, spreading his own share of flammables, made a face. "We're not children. Besides, they didn't bring us into this. We found them here."

"Hmph." Malika dusted off her hands. "That's the last of what I have."

Afsoneh wiped her forehead. The scars on her hand might never fade after what Kofi had done to her, and she would likely never gain back the full sensitivity and dexterity of those fingers. "The equipment's packed." After digging through cabinets to discover what had survived the fight, Firuz had told her to take only what was needed to make the cure, inwardly mourning the loss of everything else.

Almost everything. Malika had taken an axe to the dastgah chair upon Firuz's request, and they'd scratched runes onto the metal of the actual device to ensure it melted upon contact with heat. Holding it brought back every worst memory of their training, but they tolerated it. They had new worst memories now.

"Then it's time for the last step." Firuz looked down at the dead body Malika had left to bring back to them, roughly Kofi's size. A pang of guilt punched them in the gut—Malika would have no true ashes to give this person's family—but any other alternative was sure to put all four of them, not to mention the rest of the city's migrants, at risk. They pulled the corpse beside a workbench, the equipment already arranged to insinuate Kofi had been working.

When they stepped back, the lab was ready to burn.

Firuz stood outside the family cottage, the flames visible even though they'd waited to deactivate the clinic's fire protection runes until they were far enough away. Environmentalists were on hand in the city guard, so Firuz wasn't worried about potential damage to other structures. They had no solution for Kofi's other act of desperation though: every plant from the clinic through the Underdock had blackened, as though they, too, had been caught in the inferno. Even Kofi's green-house had been incinerated, so to speak, his months of careful work destroyed with a moment's desperation.

Firuz hoped no one and nothing else would get hurt for their mistakes. A part of them was not convinced they'd done the right thing in rejecting Kofi's offer, especially not with the fiery results, but to dwell would lead to regret, and regret helped no one.

The door behind them opened. "Firuz," said Parviz, "there's something we need to tell you."

Firuz didn't turn. The teens had listened quietly when Firuz told Malika the whole story, including the truth about their magic, trading glances Firuz saw out of the corner of their eye. It would not be the last conversation they had about this, Firuz knew, already intuiting Afsoneh would wake with even more nightmares for a long, long time.

Truth be told, so would they.

Afsoneh and Parviz came to stand on either side of them. Although the sky was heady with smoke, the flames themselves had not grown; magic users were already at work, then. If Firuz had covered their bases, which they were sure they had, investigators would find failed safeguards and an exploded experiment, and perhaps connect the nearby plant death to this test gone wrong. No one besides the four of them would ever have to know the truth of what happened, or notice missing equipment now tucked in Firuz's living room. Without the clinic's records, it would be difficult to find all the patients afflicted with the blood-bruising, but they'd do it. They'd search out every last one, and save them.

"Even though you told me not to, I've been practicing without you," blurted Afsoneh.

Firuz didn't move. "I know."

"It's my fault," said Parviz. "I was—am—so frustrated. You've promised to work on the spell for a year. Afsoneh was only trying to help."

"I figured."

"I didn't know something like the blood-bruising could happen." Anxiety twittered Afsoneh's voice. "I had no idea the entire city could be at stake."

"I know."

Parviz straightened his back, lowered his shoulders. "If you're going to be mad, be mad at me."

"I'm not mad."

"We promise to never do something like this again."

"Bacheha." A weary sigh erupted past Firuz's lips, and they took one hand from each of their siblings, looking out on a city they had tried to save, a city Kofi had almost destroyed with the same intentions. "I'm going to spend the next few weeks working on the spell. Then we'll try it. It'll be slow, and we'll have to revisit it every few months to account for new growth and how your body will shift over the next few years. And you can both be involved in the process." After all, they were unemployed now. They had all the time in the world.

The scent of smoke had reached the cottage. Gray clouds churned overhead, the tease of potential rain. If

Firuz closed their eyes, they could pretend this was an-other night in Qilwa, smelling kindled refuse from the slums, gathering their energy for another busy day at the clinic tomorrow, watching their family's antics with amused affection. They could pretend they didn't cause the death of their beloved—yes, skies, Kofi had be-come family—mentor and friend. That if they'd been honest from the start, trusted Kofi's behavior meant his acceptance, maybe they could have developed a new science together, without the dozens of deaths at their door. Maybe Firuz could have prevented all of this if they hadn't been so afraid.

Or maybe the governor would have cracked down on them and hurt the people they loved in retaliation. Useless to perseverate on decisions made long ago.

A tremor ran through Parviz's grip, up his arm, to his jaw. His gaze grew watery, and he dropped his chin. "That sounds good." He pressed his forehead into Firuz's arm. "I'm sorry I've been such an ass about it."

Not letting go of Afsoneh's hand, Firuz kissed the top of their brother's head. "I'm sorry I've been a shit sibling."

Tone a bit too bright, Afsoneh said, "At least you've been shit siblings together."

"Shit siblings, all three of us," agreed Firuz.

YEAR THREE

THE NEW CLINIC OPENED two years and one week after Firuz and their family had first arrived in Qilwa. Firuz, Afsoneh, and Parviz blended into the crowd at the opening ceremony, where the governor stood making speeches—about the tragic explosion three months ago and the loss of one of the community's fiercest advocates, a shining example of what a good Qilwan could accomplish.

"I thought she didn't even like Kofi." Afsoneh wore a rose-patterned scarf around her hair, which she'd decided to cut short into a bob and not regrow.

"She didn't," murmured Firuz. They'd taken to wearing kohl in recent weeks and found more enthusiasm for cosmetics than they would have thought. "She has to keep up appearances."

The new clinic, the governor continued, would keep its original name to honor Kofi, though Firuz knew

Kofi would have hated the starch-white awning presiding over the new building's entrance. "And though we use this time to mourn whomever we have lost, we will all move forward knowing we're continuing the good work Healer Kofi did here."

Parviz rolled his eyes. His facial hair was growing in nicely, and unlike Firuz, who had experimented with a mustache and hated it, Parviz was quite fond of his.

Firuz shook their head. "You're right. Let's get out of here."

They turned to depart from the crowd around them. "Oh," said Afsoneh. "Malika-khan told me to remind you to stop back in before we go home."

Lovely. Malika was a harsher boss than Kofi, but she was a better alternative than seeking reemployment at the clinic they'd destroyed. "She'll work me to death."

"You're not allowed to die, remember?" Parviz looked far too serious for the joke. "We still have sessions left on my chest."

"Actually," said Afsoneh, "the mortuary is the best place for you to die, though Malika-khan might dock your pay."

"Thanks," said Firuz dryly. They dug in their pockets, producing a few coins. "Why don't you two get a snack while I stop back into work?"

Afsoneh snatched up the offering. "Don't need to tell me twice. Pashmak time! C'mon, Par!"

"I hate it when you call me that," grumbled Parviz. "We'll meet you in front of the mortuary, Rooz."

Firuz shoved their hands in their pockets as they watched the two run off. Then they turned back to the clinic, where the governor had stopped speaking, was now shaking hands with the onlookers. They could have sworn they saw Ahmed's mother in the crowd, watching them; she and her wife had not taken Firuz before a magistrate, and with the fire, the investigation into them had dropped. Guilt at their inability to save Ahmed still haunted them, and his mother's presence was no comfort. But so, too, were other patients they or Kofi had treated present, milling about to take in his legacy.

Kofi was dead, his mistakes only named such by a background Firuz was no longer sure had served them. Still, Firuz had made their choice, and Kofi had died, and that meant Sassanian migrants no longer had a safe haven, a clinic to call their own. But Malika's mortuary was free from the governor's oversight, and Firuz's name was known enough that people came in at odd hours, looking for help. And when they had extra coin, Firuz put it away to save up for their own clinic one day, one the governor would have no hold over. One to truly mark this city as their home and honor Kofi and all he'd tried to do, the misguided and the well-intentioned alike. A tribute to a desperate man trying to do his best by the people he loved.

A wry smile on their face, Firuz headed back to work.

AFTERWORD

W HEN I WAS A CHILD, my father instilled a fierce pride about our heritage in me. The Persians, he told me, had one of the largest empires in the world, spanning through centuries and millennia. We came from those folk, as both of my parents immigrated to the United States from Iran. To be Persian was to embrace this legacy of empire with pride because despite everyone who tried to wipe us out—the Muslim Arabs, the Mongols, the British and French and Russians—we are still here.

It did not occur to me to be ashamed until my second master's program, when I sat in a postcolonial literature class and realized I was living the legacy of empire in my daily life. Having been born and raised and now studying on stolen land, with a professor whose family had been caught in India's partition, and being one of the few people of color in the department—all of these and more made me realize the empire I had long admired could not be divorced from these modern contexts either, despite their seeming dissimilarities. It didn't matter that Persepolis was not built by African slaves; many Black Iranians are a legacy of the other dynasties that used them. It didn't matter that Persians had invented algebra or been the founders of modern medicine or had written one of the longest epics in world literature. What did such accomplishments mean when there were still subjugated people under our care?

But what did it also mean that while we had once been an empire, we were now a hated people?

After the Muslim conquest of Iran, the majority of the country converted for fear of subjugation and violence. Those that did not, despite the persecution, hid their native Zoroastrian practices—a tradition stretching back to the time of Cyrus the Great—and those who would not hide or convert fled to India, to become modern Parsees. Farsi, as a language, was almost wiped out in place of Arabic, until Abolqasem Ferdowsi penned the Persian Book of Kings, the *Shahnameh*, an epic of about 50,000 couplets—over double the length of the *Iliad* and *Odyssey* combined.

Fast-forward to the nineteenth century, where countries like Russia and France and England set their sights on the oil-rich country of Iran. Fast-forward to the twentieth, where the United States feared a socialist democracy in Iran spelled doom for their foreign interests, and sent the CIA to help instigate a coup.

Fast-forward to 2016, when Donald Trump was elected president of the United States and a ban against Muslim-majority countries was instated. Fast-forward to 2021, where U.S. senator Susan Collins, in response to the storming of the White House, wrote in an op-ed for the *Bangor Daily News*, "My first thought was that the Iranians had followed through on their threat to strike the Capitol."

What does it mean to be oppressed when you were once an oppressor?

I did not initially set out to write *The Bruising of Qilwa* to explore these issues. Initially, I was trying to use my background a scientist to learn how to write a short story, intending it to be a medical fantasy. But as Firuz began unraveling the mystery of the blood-bruising, so, too, did they have to contend with their role as a Sassanian in Qilwa.

I had initially designed the queendom of Dilmun, the country which Firuz called home for most of their life, as an allegory for the Muslim conquest of Iran, but with the idea of what Iran might have looked like if the invaders had never been expelled. Since then, as all stories do, these countries and peoples have morphed to become their own, but I continued to pose to myself the question I still do not have an answer for: what does it mean that today, the people from whom my parents came from are vilified and hated in the country in which we live, but once, however long ago, these same people subjugated others?

Firuz is not a hero, and Kofi is not a villain. Their ideological clash ends in violence, as so many often do, but Firuz does not come away with the triumphant knowledge that they won. They didn't win. As they began the story, so they conclude it: a marginalized person in a country afraid of its own recolonization.

As a multi-marginalized person in the United States, I think a lot about this country's treatment of the Other and the ways in which this country was built on the backs of those very people. And though I can trace the historical, social, and cultural factors from which many of today's issues stem, I come back again to the same fear of the Other: a fear of resource loss, of morality loss, of dignity loss. An actual rather than imagined reality for so many people who live in this country today, including over 11 million undocumented immigrants, and so many more who are willing to feel that ostracism in the hopes of achieving a different and better future for their families.

While I only touched on some of these issues in *The Bruising of Qilwa*, I hope it will inspire a conversation about all the ways in which individuals can put aside their judgments and join migrants and other marginalized people to create a brighter tomorrow, rather than perpetuate a nation's fears of drowning under the depth of a short but fraught history.

And I hope this story can inspire a little more nuance in these conversations, too.

— Naseem Jamnia
August 2022
Written on traditional Numu, Wašiw, Newe, and Nuwu territories

ACKNOWLEDGMENTS

A book, as the illusive "everyone" says, does not happen by one person but by everyone who crosses its path. This book is no different, as it never would have taken shape without so much love and support and hard work by others.

First, thank you to my agent, Erica Bauman, who has fought tirelessly for my work from the get-go, who knows and encourages my ambitions and is the best business, editorial, and creative partner I could ask for. Thank you for always having my back.

Next, thank you to the team at Tachyon: Jacob Weisman, Jaymee Goh, Jill Roberts, Rick Klaw, and Kasey Lansdale. Thank you for believing in this story, shepherding it into the world, and working tirelessly on its behalf. My magnificent cover cover and interior design came from the brilliant Elizabeth Story; I am still in awe of it. I am also so, so grateful to Shailja Patel and Kaveh Akbar for allowing their words to grace the beginning of this book. Thank you both for writing works that delight and inspire me.

Thank you to the Fall 2019 705 workshop, who read and critiqued the short story version of *Qilwa*, including my thesis advisor, David Anthony Durham. Thanks to Zelda Knight at *Aurelia Leo* for publishing this earlier version, "Nothing Less Than Bones." *Qilwa* was also greatly affected by my classwork with Drs. Guadalupe Escobar, Nasia Anam, and Emily Hobson. Thanks also to Christopher Coake, who threatened to dance around his office when he heard the news of this book's imminent publication.

My MFA/UNR cohort has become family to me. December Cuccaro, from whom I've been inseparable since 2019: thank you for everything, from introducing me to *Dragon Age* (you're welcome for *Persona*) to being there whenever I needed you; please forever continue to laugh at my terrible combat skills. Phoebe Wagner: I cannot thank you enough for being there for me, from my first foray into submission hell to that one semester (you know the one) and beyond. Andy Butter: will probably never stop calling you Butter Boi, tbh. Thanks also to those outside the cohort, who have been enthusiastic and supportive even when they've had tough things going on in their own lives: Michelle Aucion Wait, Bryant Wait, Cameron Gibson, Linzy Garcia, Leanne Howard, Emily Sawan, Molly Beckwith,

Renee Christopher, Brontë Wieland, Andrew Dincher, and David Gomez. Morgan Dunwoodie: thank you for your constant belief that *something* of mine would get picked up.

Thanks to my many writing communities, including the 2019 Lambda Literary Fellows, 2022 Debuts group, and the rainbow pub. I'm sure I'll miss people, but thanks to those who have particularly supported this book's journey: Charlie Jane Anders, Shannon Chakraborty, R. B. Lemberg, Sam J. Miller, Amelie Wan Zhao, Rebecca Mix, Neon Yang, Z.R. Ellor, and Ray Stoeve. A huge shout-out to Melissa Brinks and Zora Gilbert, who held down the fort at Sidequest. Zone while I was doing my MFA and working on this book, and to Kay Allen, Jessie Ulmer, and Monica Robinson at Sword & Kettle Press for their excitement and voting on my title choices.

My friends "back home" have been invaluable support along the way: Misha and Elise Grifka Wander, Jennie Kaplan, Alison Thumel, Katherine Brandt, Karis Rogerson, and Emmy Colón-Geistlinger. To my mother-in-law, Liliana Bilbao: thank you for being supportive not only of my marriage (ha!) but also of my artistic endeavors. To my undergrad mentors, Vu Tran and Rachel DeWoskin: thank you for all you taught me and for encouraging me to pursue my writing seriously.

To Beth Kopsa Gibbs: I promised you the first day of freshman year Brit Lit that I'd publish my books. It took over 15 years, but here I am.

To Terry J. Benton-Walker: WE DID IT!!! My first book is here, and yours comes out soon, and I am so, so proud of us for sticking together through everything. You're the truest friend I could have ever asked for, and I love you so much. I can't wait until everyone gets to meet Cris and Clem and Alex and Loren and Mags and love them as much as I do. Thank you for being there for every tear and every joy. I could not be here without you.

To my family, who has been here from the beginning: Maman, thank you for understanding why I had to leave the sciences even when doing so broke both of our hearts. Baba, thank you for always encouraging my writing. Seena, I hope you're proud of me.

To Gabe, without whom none of this would be possible: I love you so much. Thank you for being my fiercest advocate and reader (and harshest critic!) and for making it possible for me to pursue the dream I've had since I was nine.

Finally, to everyone who picked up this book: thank you for spending time with Firuz and their family. They appreciate it, and so do I.

Naseem Jamnia is a former neuroscientist and recent MFA graduate from the University of Nevada, Reno. Their work has appeared in the *Washington Post*, *Cosmopolitan*, *The Rumpus*, *The Writer's Chronicle*, and other venues.

Jamnia has been awarded fellowships from Bitch Media, Lambda Literary, and Otherwise, including the inaugural Samuel R. Delany Fellowship.

In addition to cowriting the academic text *Positive Interactions with At-Risk Children* (Routledge, 2019), Jamnia's work has been included in the Lambda Literary *EMERGE* anthology (2020) and *We Made Uranium! And Other True Stories from the University of Chicago's Extraordinary Scavenger Hunt* (University of Chicago, 2019).

Jamnia is the managing editor at Sword & Kettle

Press, an independent publishing house of inclusive feminist speculative fiction. They are also the former managing editor at Sidequest.Zone, an independent gaming criticism website.

A Persian-Chicagoan and child to Iranian immigrants, Jamnia now lives in Reno with their husband, dog, and two cats.

Find out at more at www.naseemwrites.com or on Twitter and Instagram @jamsternazzy.